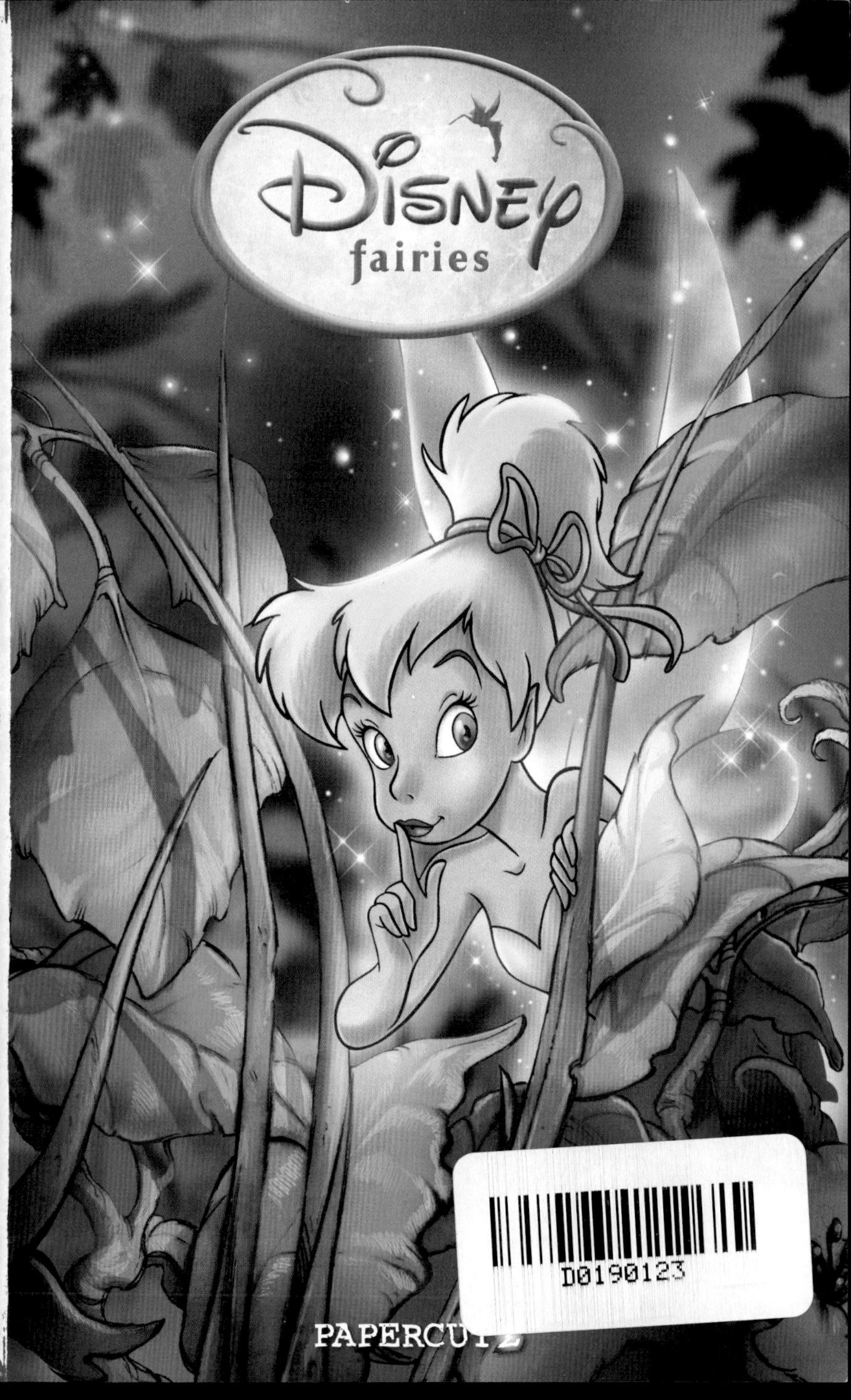
Disney
fairies
PAPERCU

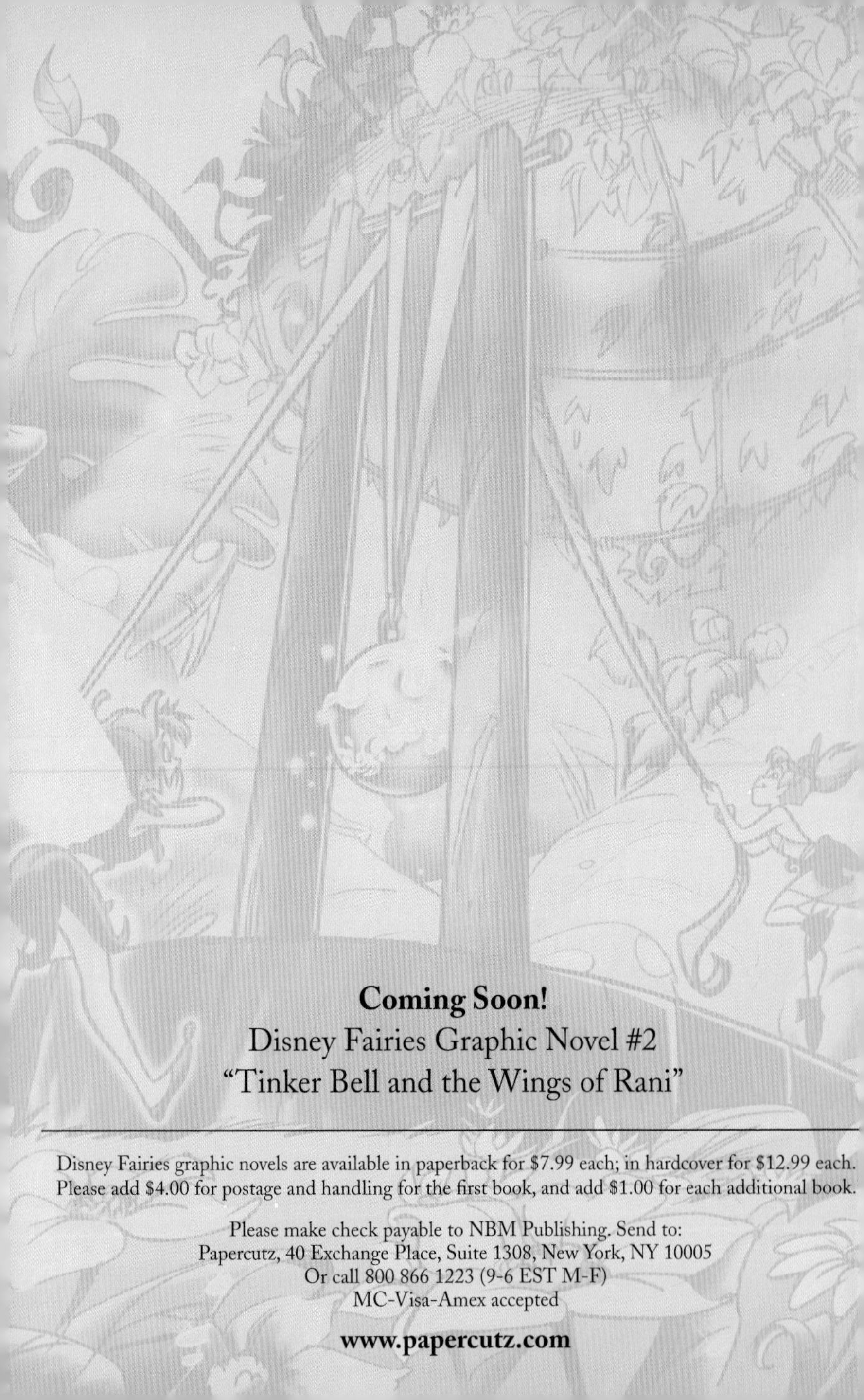

Coming Soon!

Disney Fairies Graphic Novel #2

"Tinker Bell and the Wings of Rani"

Disney Fairies graphic novels are available in paperback for $7.99 each; in hardcover for $12.99 each. Please add $4.00 for postage and handling for the first book, and add $1.00 for each additional book.

Please make check payable to NBM Publishing. Send to:
Papercutz, 40 Exchange Place, Suite 1308, New York, NY 10005
Or call 800 866 1223 (9-6 EST M-F)
MC-Visa-Amex accepted

www.papercutz.com

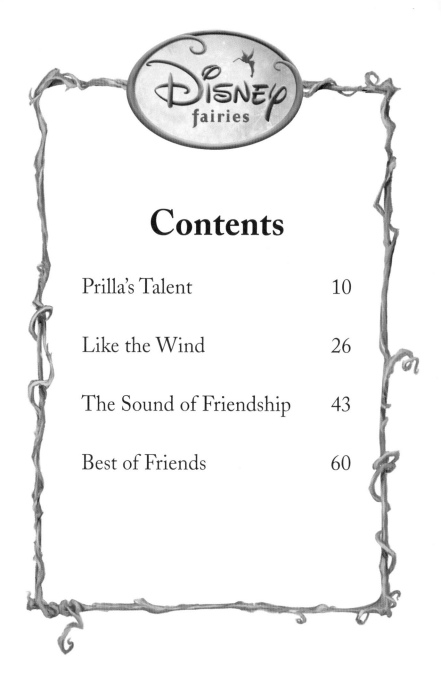

Contents

"Prilla's Talent"
Script: Bruno Enna
Revised Dialogue: Stefan Petrucha
Pencils: Giada Perissinotto
Inks: Marina Baggio, Roberta Zanotta
Lettering: Janice Chiang
Page 5 Art:
Pencils: Elena Pianta
Inks: Roberta Zanotta
Color: Federico Bertolucci

"Like the Wind"
Script: Augusto Macchetto
Revised Dialogue: Stefan Petrucha
Pencils: Giada Perissinotto
Inks: Roberta Zanotta
Color: Litomilano
Lettering: Janice Chiang
Page 26 Concept and layout: Giovanni Rigano
Clean up: Manuela Razzi
Inks: Marina Baggio
Color: Federico Bertolucci

"The Sound of Friendship"
Script: Giulia Conti
Revised Dialogue: Stefan Petrucha
Layout: Emilio Urbano
Clean up: Manuela Razzi
Inks: Marina Baggio
Color: Litomilano
Lettering: Janice Chiang
Page 43 Art: Manuela Razzi
Inks: Marina Baggio
Color: Andrea Cago

"Best of Friends"
Script: Augusto Macchetto
Revised Dialogue: Stefan Petrucha
Pencils: Caterina Giorgetti
Inks: Roberta Zanotta
Color: Lito Milano
Lettering: Janice Chiang
Page 60 Art:
Pencils: Emilio Urbano and Manuela Razzi
Inks: Marina Baggio
Color: Andrea Cagol

Chris Nelson and Shelly Dutchak – Production
Michael Petranek – Editorial Assistant
Jim Salicrup - Editor-in-Chief

ISBN: 978-1-59707-186-4 paperback edition
ISBN: 978-1-59707-187-1 hardcover edition

Printed in Singapore. January 2010
by Tien Wah Press PTE LTD
4 Pandan Crescent
Singapore 128475

Distributed by Macmillan.
10 9 8 7 6 5 4 3 2 1

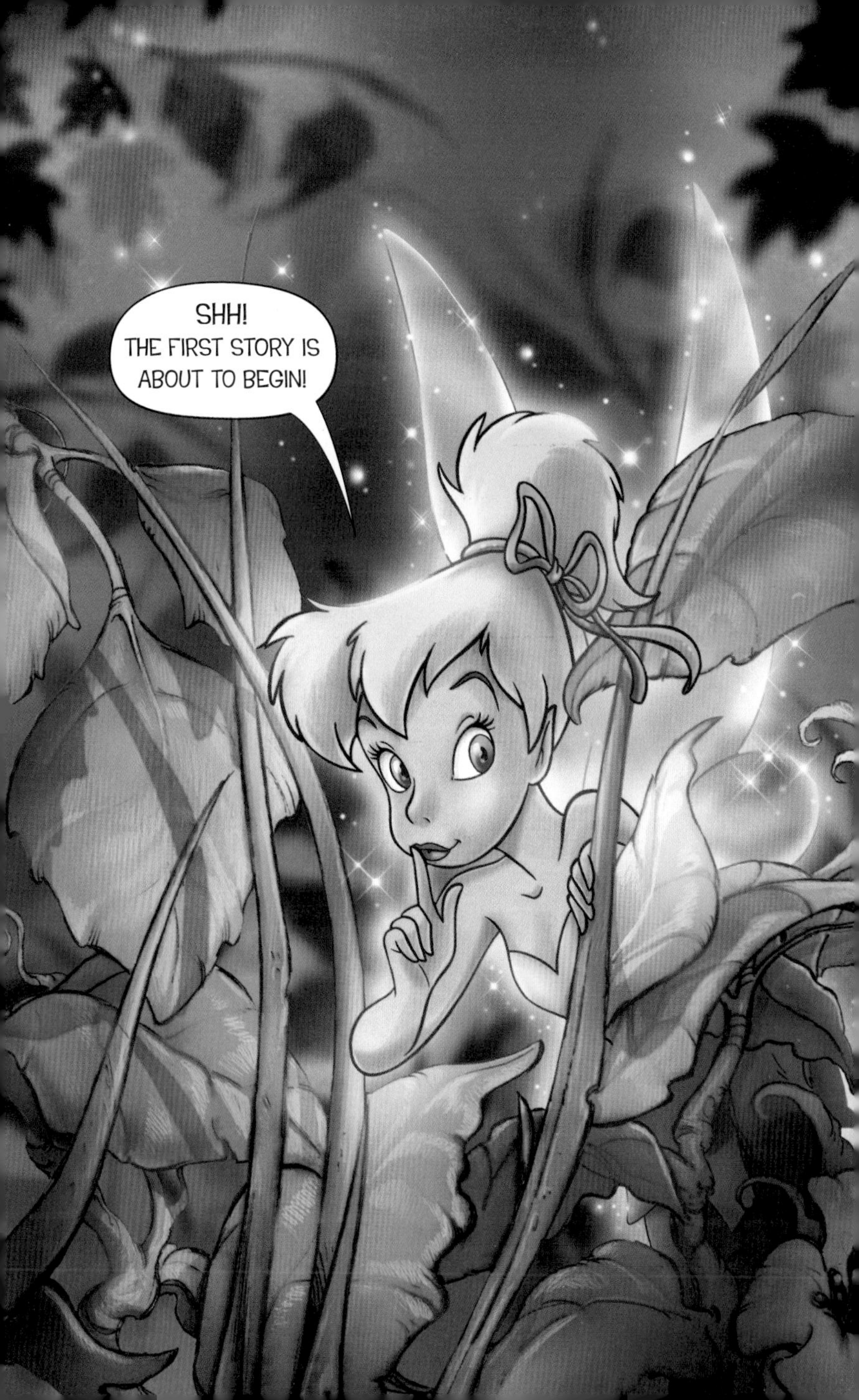
SHH!
THE FIRST STORY IS
ABOUT TO BEGIN!

Welcome to the
World of Disney Fairies

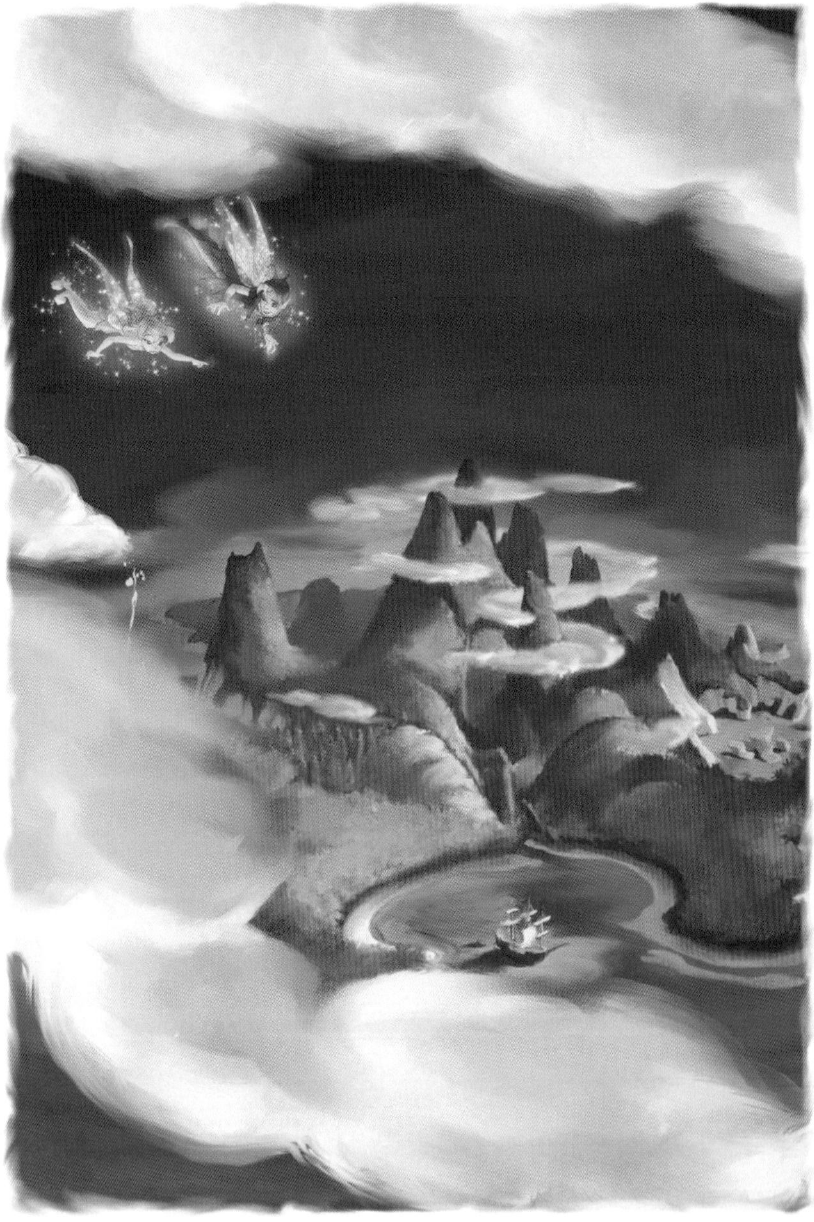

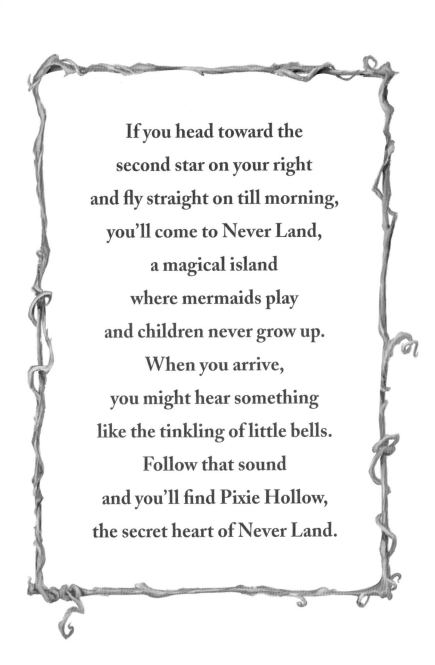

If you head toward the
second star on your right
and fly straight on till morning,
you'll come to Never Land,
a magical island
where mermaids play
and children never grow up.
When you arrive,
you might hear something
like the tinkling of little bells.
Follow that sound
and you'll find Pixie Hollow,
the secret heart of Never Land.

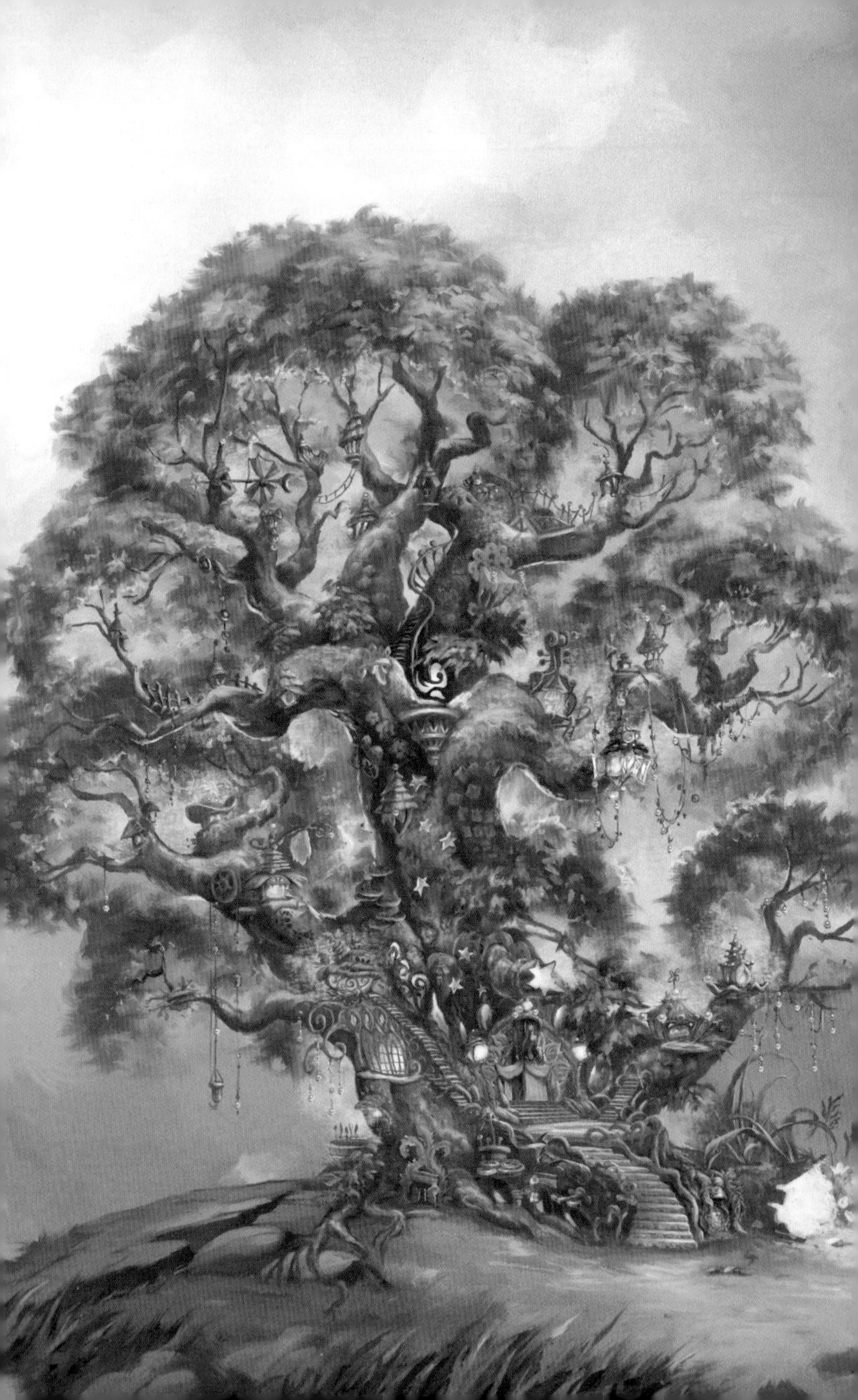

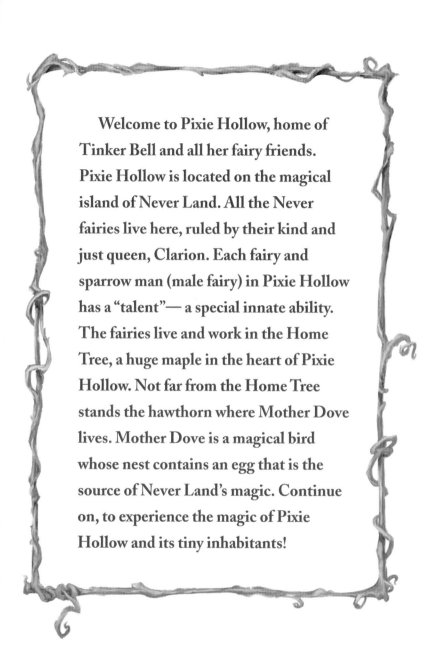

Welcome to Pixie Hollow, home of Tinker Bell and all her fairy friends. Pixie Hollow is located on the magical island of Never Land. All the Never fairies live here, ruled by their kind and just queen, Clarion. Each fairy and sparrow man (male fairy) in Pixie Hollow has a "talent"— a special innate ability. The fairies live and work in the Home Tree, a huge maple in the heart of Pixie Hollow. Not far from the Home Tree stands the hawthorn where Mother Dove lives. Mother Dove is a magical bird whose nest contains an egg that is the source of Never Land's magic. Continue on, to experience the magic of Pixie Hollow and its tiny inhabitants!

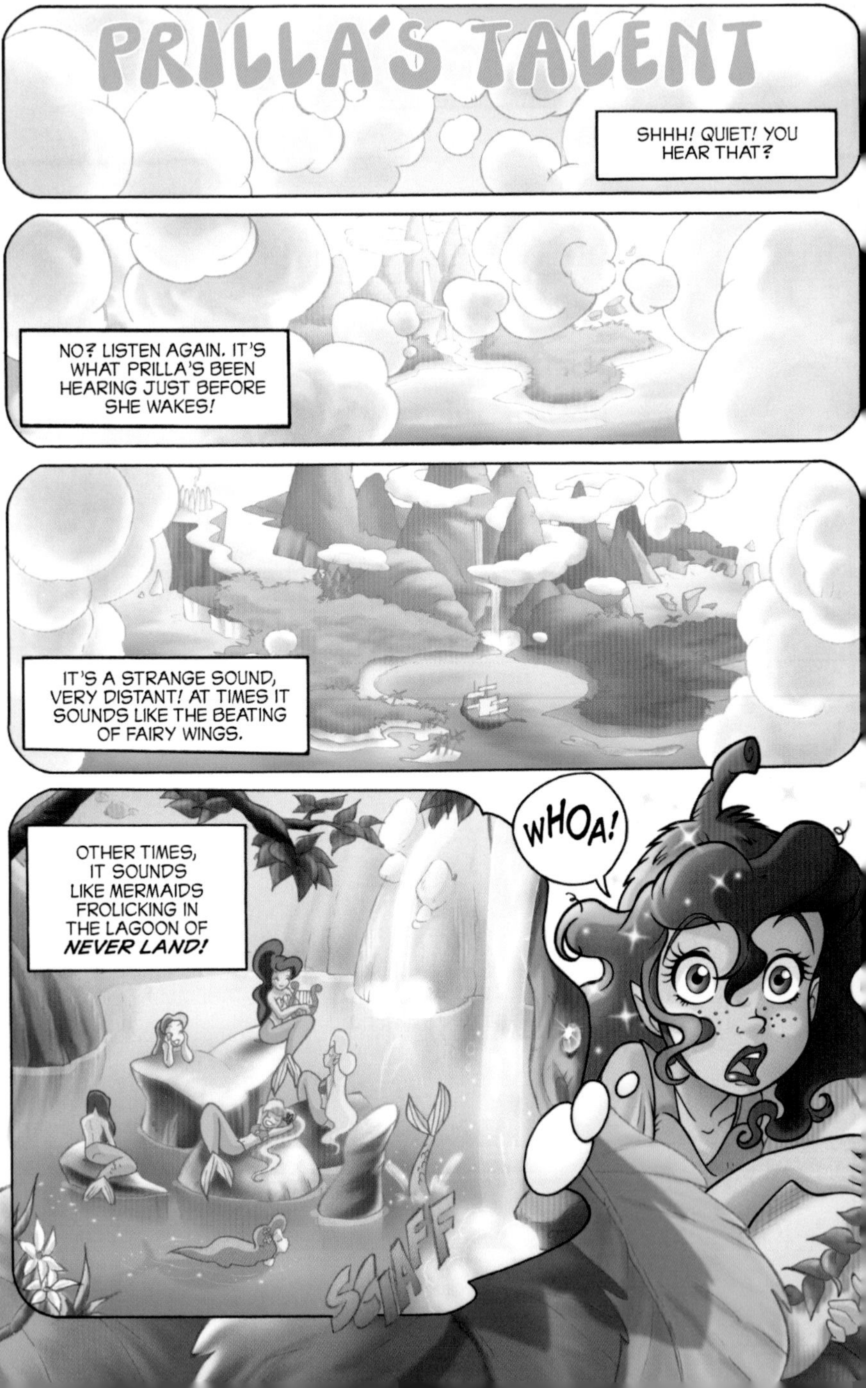
PRILLA'S TALENT
SHHH! QUIET! YOU HEAR THAT?
NO? LISTEN AGAIN. IT'S WHAT PRILLA'S BEEN HEARING JUST BEFORE SHE WAKES!
IT'S A STRANGE SOUND, VERY DISTANT! AT TIMES IT SOUNDS LIKE THE BEATING OF FAIRY WINGS.
OTHER TIMES, IT SOUNDS LIKE MERMAIDS FROLICKING IN THE LAGOON OF *NEVER LAND!*
WHOA!
SPLAFF

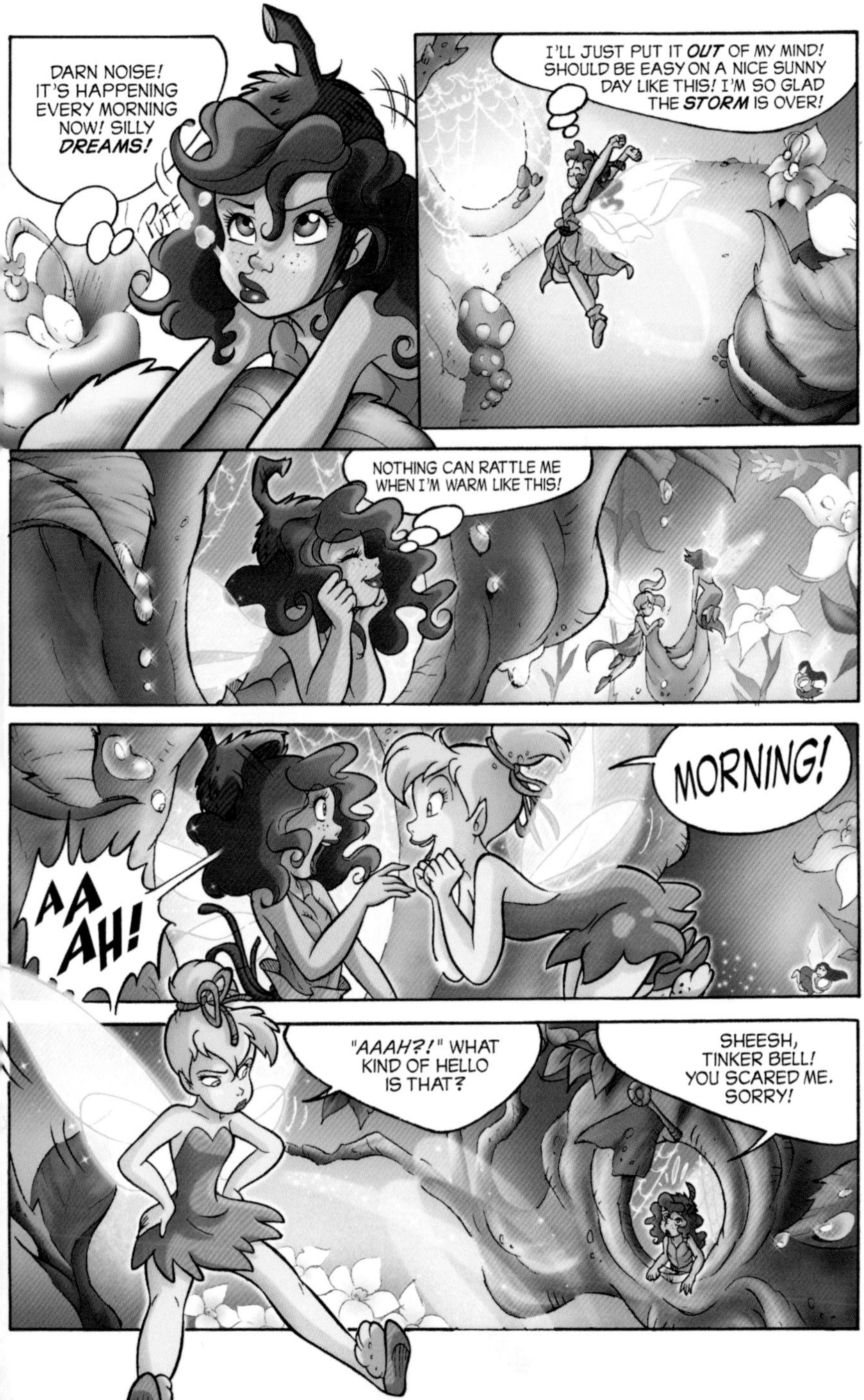
DARN NOISE! IT'S HAPPENING EVERY MORNING NOW! SILLY DREAMS!
PUFF
I'LL JUST PUT IT OUT OF MY MIND! SHOULD BE EASY ON A NICE SUNNY DAY LIKE THIS! I'M SO GLAD THE STORM IS OVER!
NOTHING CAN RATTLE ME WHEN I'M WARM LIKE THIS!
MORNING!
AAAH!
"AAAH?!" WHAT KIND OF HELLO IS THAT?
SHEESH, TINKER BELL! YOU SCARED ME. SORRY!

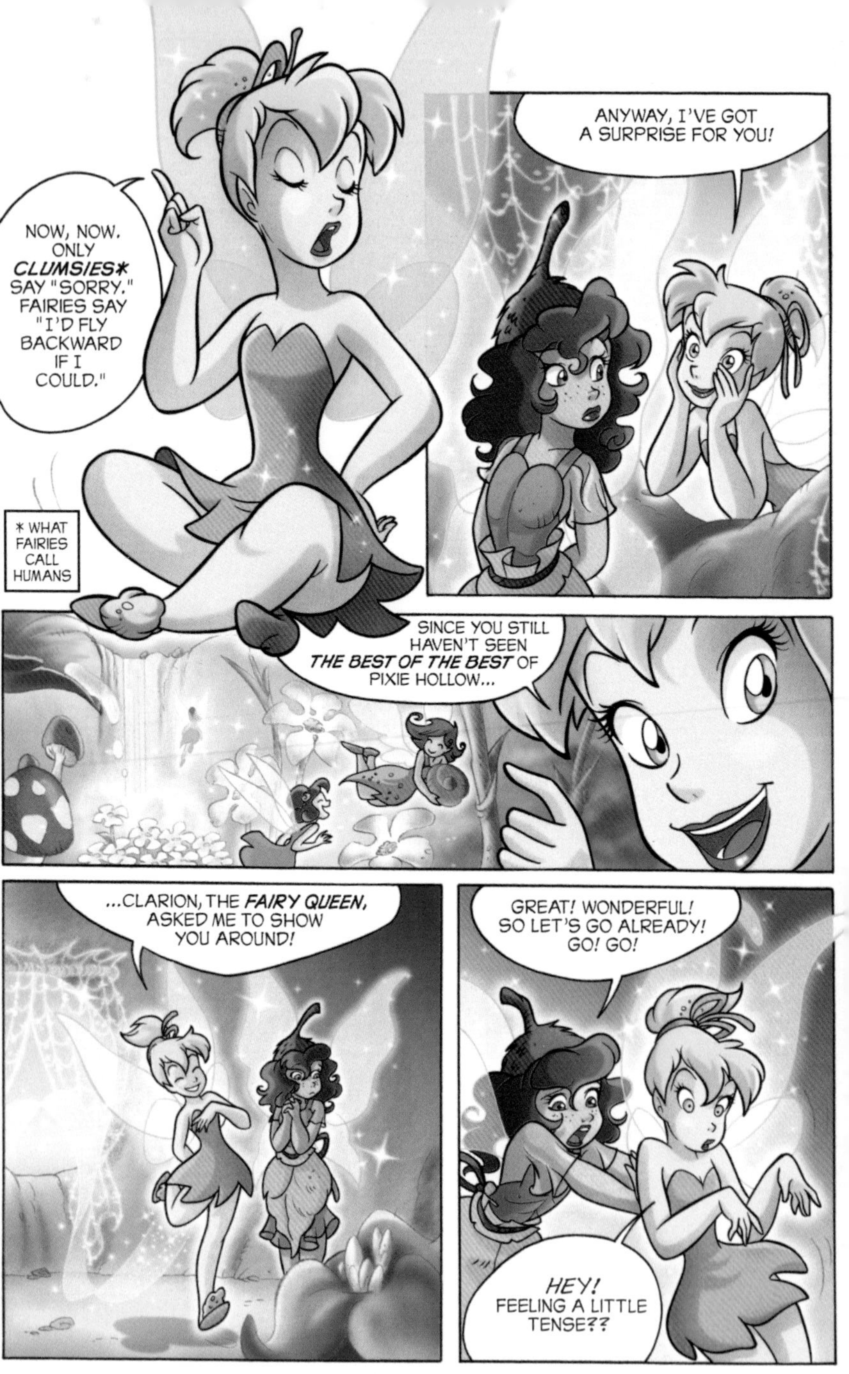
NOW, NOW. ONLY ***CLUMSIES**** SAY "SORRY." FAIRIES SAY "I'D FLY BACKWARD IF I COULD."
* WHAT FAIRIES CALL HUMANS
ANYWAY, I'VE GOT A SURPRISE FOR YOU!
SINCE YOU STILL HAVEN'T SEEN ***THE BEST OF THE BEST*** OF PIXIE HOLLOW...
...CLARION, THE ***FAIRY QUEEN,*** ASKED ME TO SHOW YOU AROUND!
GREAT! WONDERFUL! SO LET'S GO ALREADY! GO! GO!
HEY! FEELING A LITTLE TENSE??

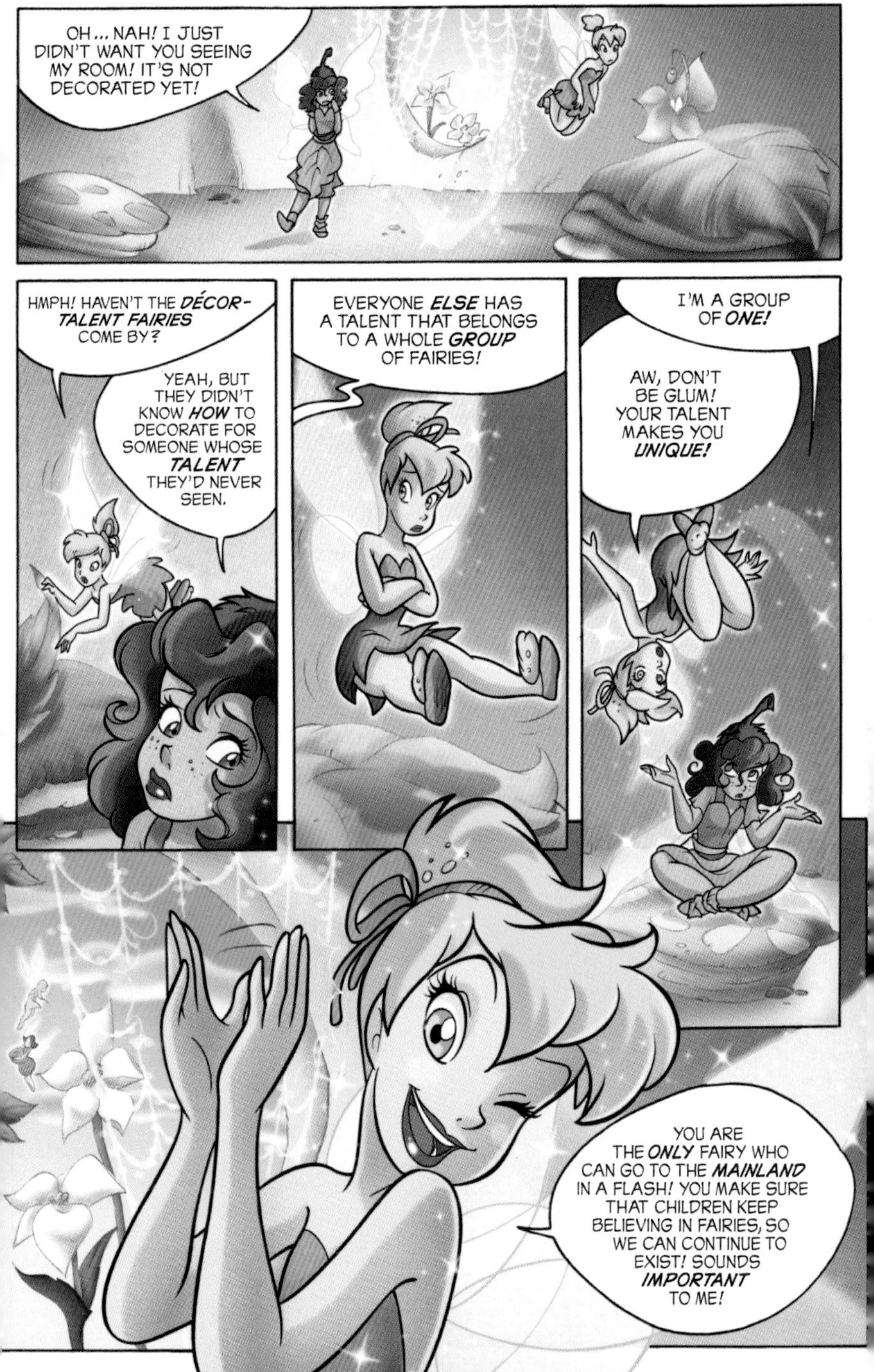
OH... NAH! I JUST DIDN'T WANT YOU SEEING MY ROOM! IT'S NOT DECORATED YET!
HMPH! HAVEN'T THE DÉCOR-TALENT FAIRIES COME BY?
YEAH, BUT THEY DIDN'T KNOW HOW TO DECORATE FOR SOMEONE WHOSE TALENT THEY'D NEVER SEEN.
EVERYONE ELSE HAS A TALENT THAT BELONGS TO A WHOLE GROUP OF FAIRIES!
I'M A GROUP OF ONE!
AW, DON'T BE GLUM! YOUR TALENT MAKES YOU UNIQUE!
YOU ARE THE ONLY FAIRY WHO CAN GO TO THE MAINLAND IN A FLASH! YOU MAKE SURE THAT CHILDREN KEEP BELIEVING IN FAIRIES, SO WE CAN CONTINUE TO EXIST! SOUNDS IMPORTANT TO ME!

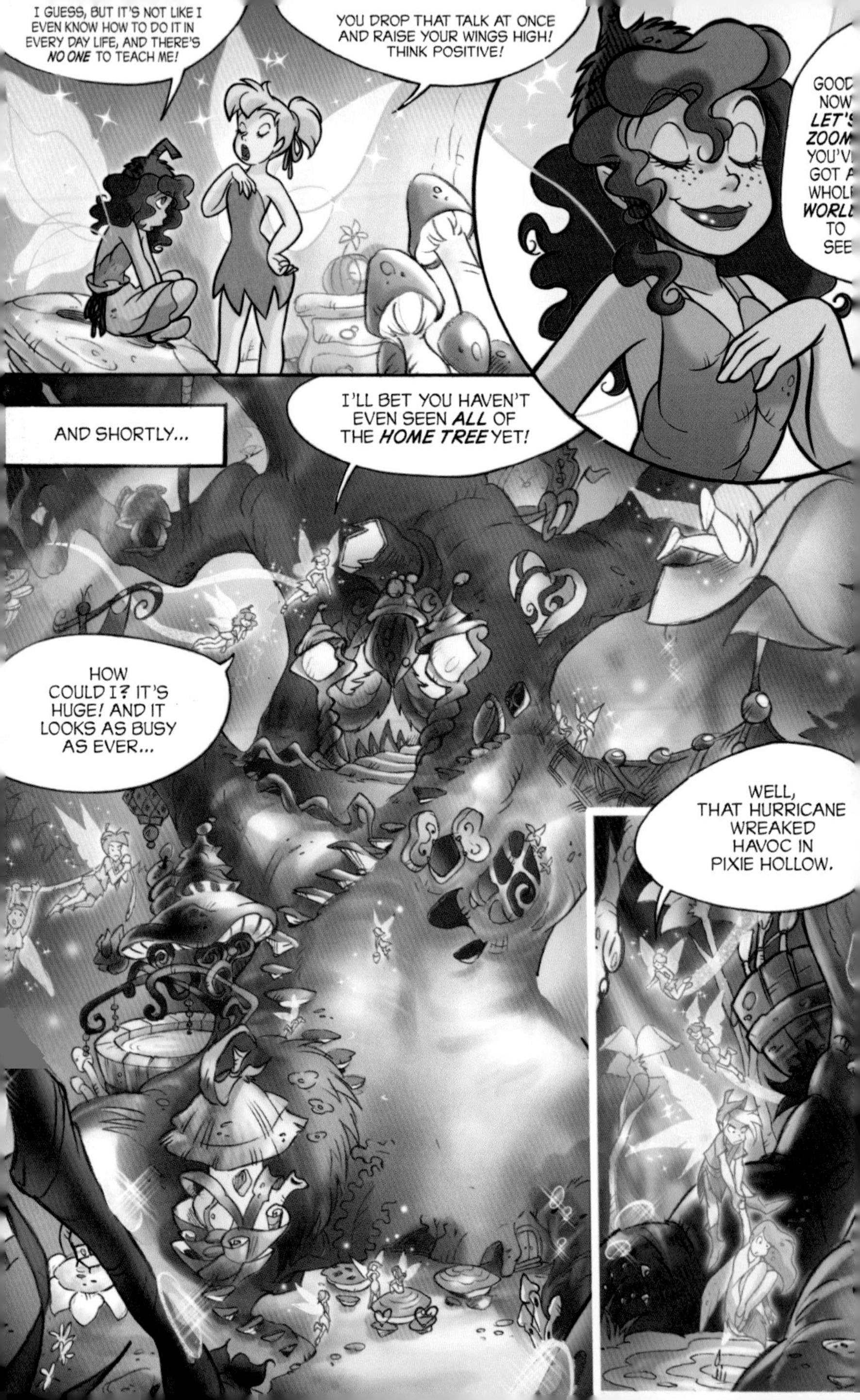

I GUESS, BUT IT'S NOT LIKE I EVEN KNOW HOW TO DO IT IN EVERY DAY LIFE, AND THERE'S *NO ONE* TO TEACH ME!
YOU DROP THAT TALK AT ONCE AND RAISE YOUR WINGS HIGH! THINK POSITIVE!
GOOD NOW *LET'S ZOOM* YOU'V GOT A WHOL *WORL* TO SEE
AND SHORTLY...
I'LL BET YOU HAVEN'T EVEN SEEN *ALL* OF THE *HOME TREE* YET!
HOW COULD I? IT'S HUGE! AND IT LOOKS AS BUSY AS EVER...
WELL, THAT HURRICANE WREAKED HAVOC IN PIXIE HOLLOW.

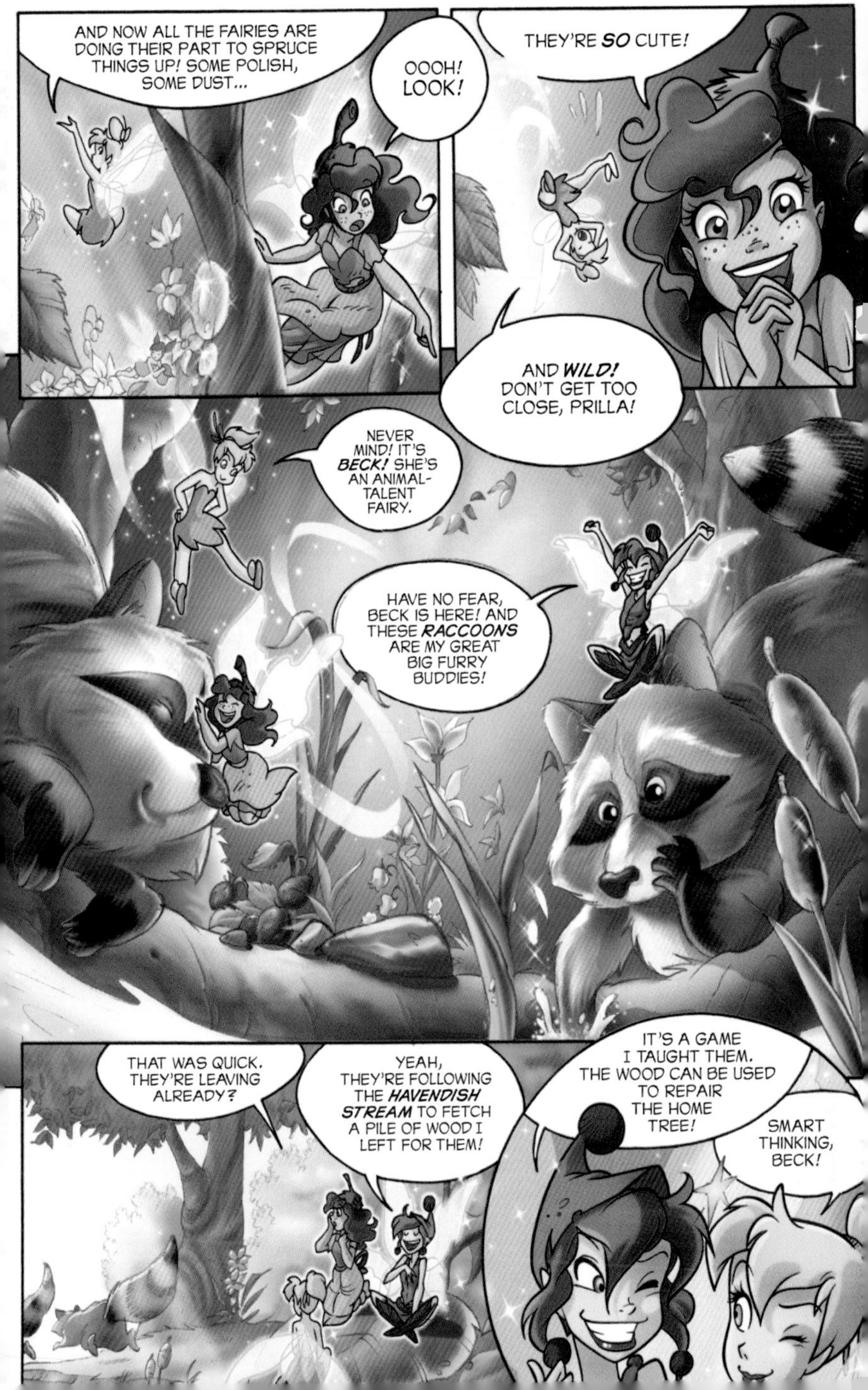
AND NOW ALL THE FAIRIES ARE DOING THEIR PART TO SPRUCE THINGS UP! SOME POLISH, SOME DUST...
OOOH! LOOK!
THEY'RE **SO** CUTE!
AND **WILD!** DON'T GET TOO CLOSE, PRILLA!
NEVER MIND! IT'S **BECK!** SHE'S AN ANIMAL-TALENT FAIRY.
HAVE NO FEAR, BECK IS HERE! AND THESE **RACCOONS** ARE MY GREAT BIG FURRY BUDDIES!
THAT WAS QUICK. THEY'RE LEAVING ALREADY?
YEAH, THEY'RE FOLLOWING THE **HAVENDISH STREAM** TO FETCH A PILE OF WOOD I LEFT FOR THEM!
IT'S A GAME I TAUGHT THEM. THE WOOD CAN BE USED TO REPAIR THE HOME TREE!
SMART THINKING, BECK!

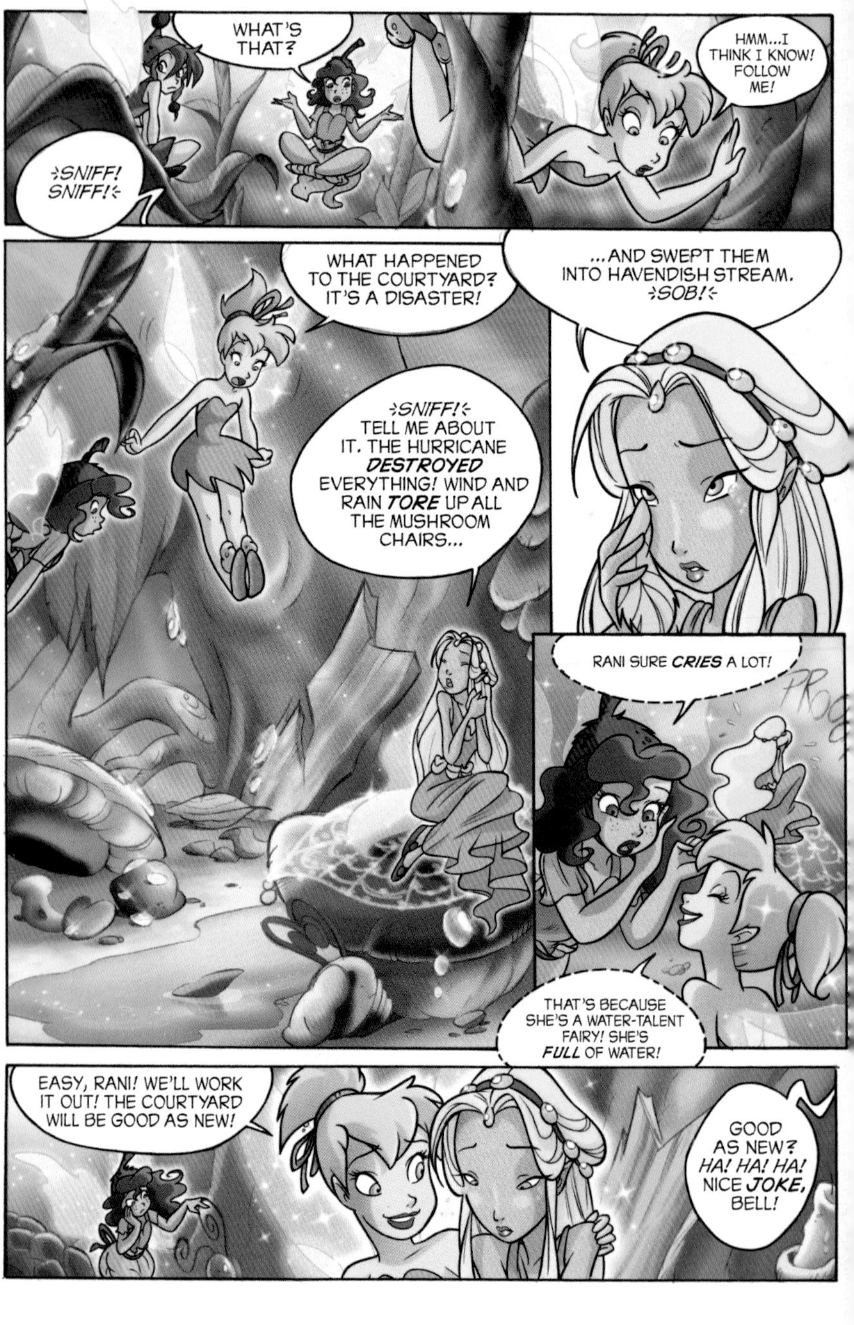
WHAT'S THAT?
⸗SNIFF! SNIFF!⸗
HMM...I THINK I KNOW! FOLLOW ME!
WHAT HAPPENED TO THE COURTYARD? IT'S A DISASTER!
⸗SNIFF!⸗ TELL ME ABOUT IT. THE HURRICANE *DESTROYED* EVERYTHING! WIND AND RAIN *TORE* UP ALL THE MUSHROOM CHAIRS...
...AND SWEPT THEM INTO HAVENDISH STREAM. ⸗SOB!⸗
RANI SURE *CRIES* A LOT!
THAT'S BECAUSE SHE'S A WATER-TALENT FAIRY! SHE'S *FULL* OF WATER!
EASY, RANI! WE'LL WORK IT OUT! THE COURTYARD WILL BE GOOD AS NEW!
GOOD AS NEW? *HA! HA! HA!* NICE *JOKE,* BELL!

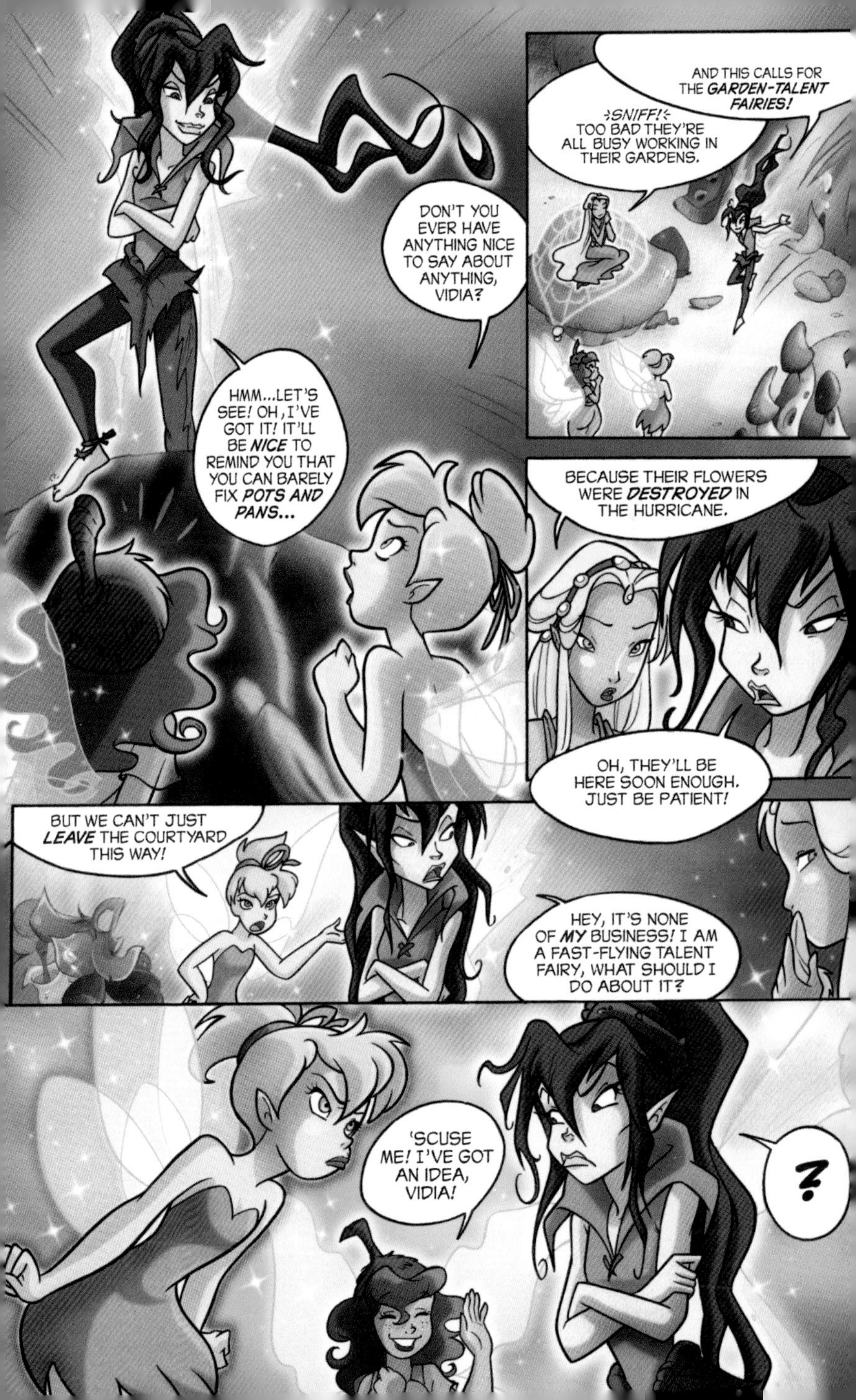

DON'T YOU EVER HAVE ANYTHING NICE TO SAY ABOUT ANYTHING, VIDIA?
HMM...LET'S SEE! OH, I'VE GOT IT! IT'LL BE NICE TO REMIND YOU THAT YOU CAN BARELY FIX POTS AND PANS...
AND THIS CALLS FOR THE GARDEN-TALENT FAIRIES!
SNIFF! TOO BAD THEY'RE ALL BUSY WORKING IN THEIR GARDENS.
BECAUSE THEIR FLOWERS WERE DESTROYED IN THE HURRICANE.
OH, THEY'LL BE HERE SOON ENOUGH. JUST BE PATIENT!
BUT WE CAN'T JUST LEAVE THE COURTYARD THIS WAY!
HEY, IT'S NONE OF MY BUSINESS! I AM A FAST-FLYING TALENT FAIRY, WHAT SHOULD I DO ABOUT IT?
'SCUSE ME! I'VE GOT AN IDEA, VIDIA!
?

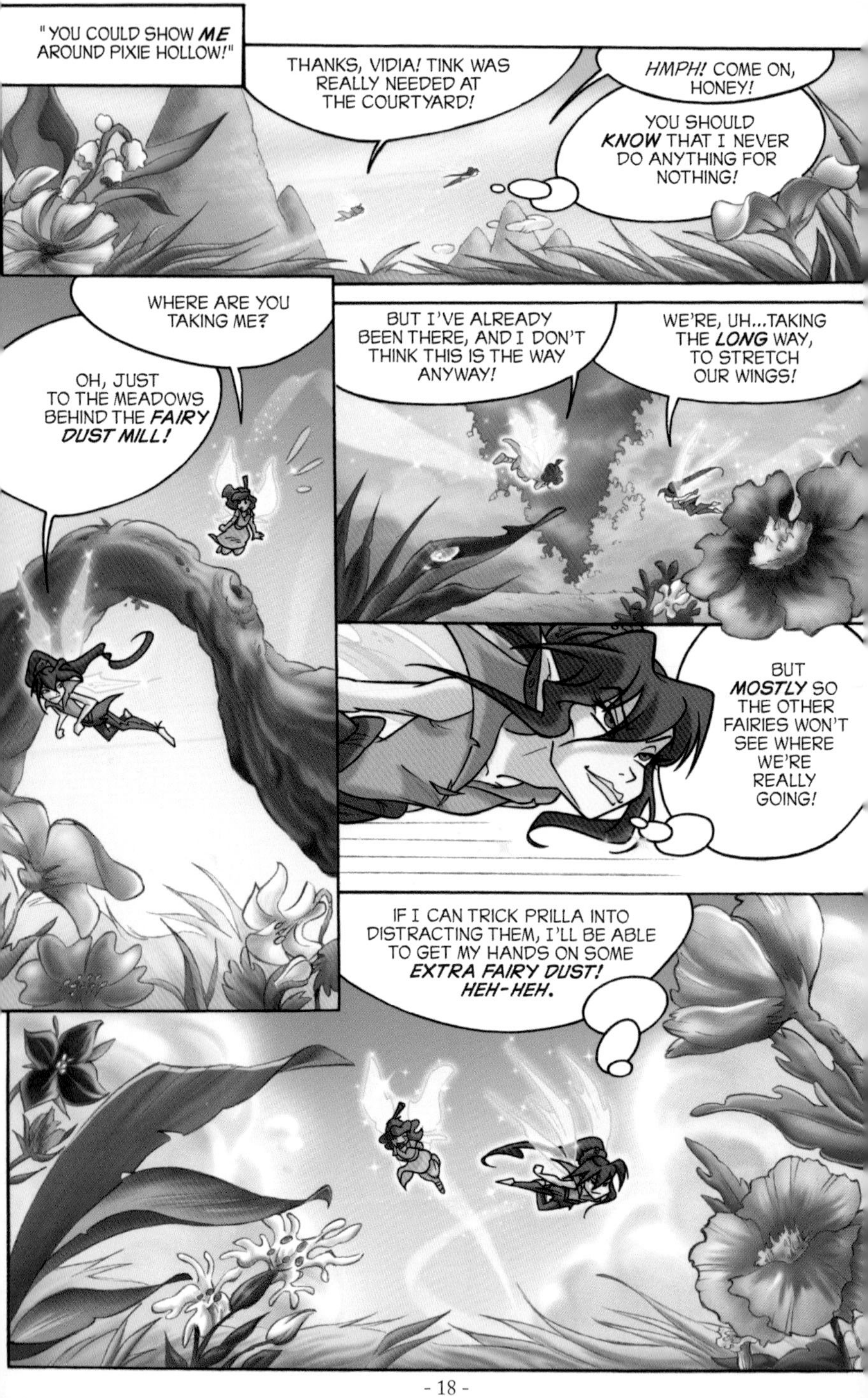

"YOU COULD SHOW *ME* AROUND PIXIE HOLLOW!"
THANKS, VIDIA! TINK WAS REALLY NEEDED AT THE COURTYARD!
HMPH! COME ON, HONEY!
YOU SHOULD *KNOW* THAT I NEVER DO ANYTHING FOR NOTHING!
WHERE ARE YOU TAKING ME?
OH, JUST TO THE MEADOWS BEHIND THE *FAIRY DUST MILL!*
BUT I'VE ALREADY BEEN THERE, AND I DON'T THINK THIS IS THE WAY ANYWAY!
WE'RE, UH...TAKING THE *LONG* WAY, TO STRETCH OUR WINGS!
BUT *MOSTLY* SO THE OTHER FAIRIES WON'T SEE WHERE WE'RE REALLY GOING!
IF I CAN TRICK PRILLA INTO DISTRACTING THEM, I'LL BE ABLE TO GET MY HANDS ON SOME *EXTRA FAIRY DUST! HEH-HEH.*

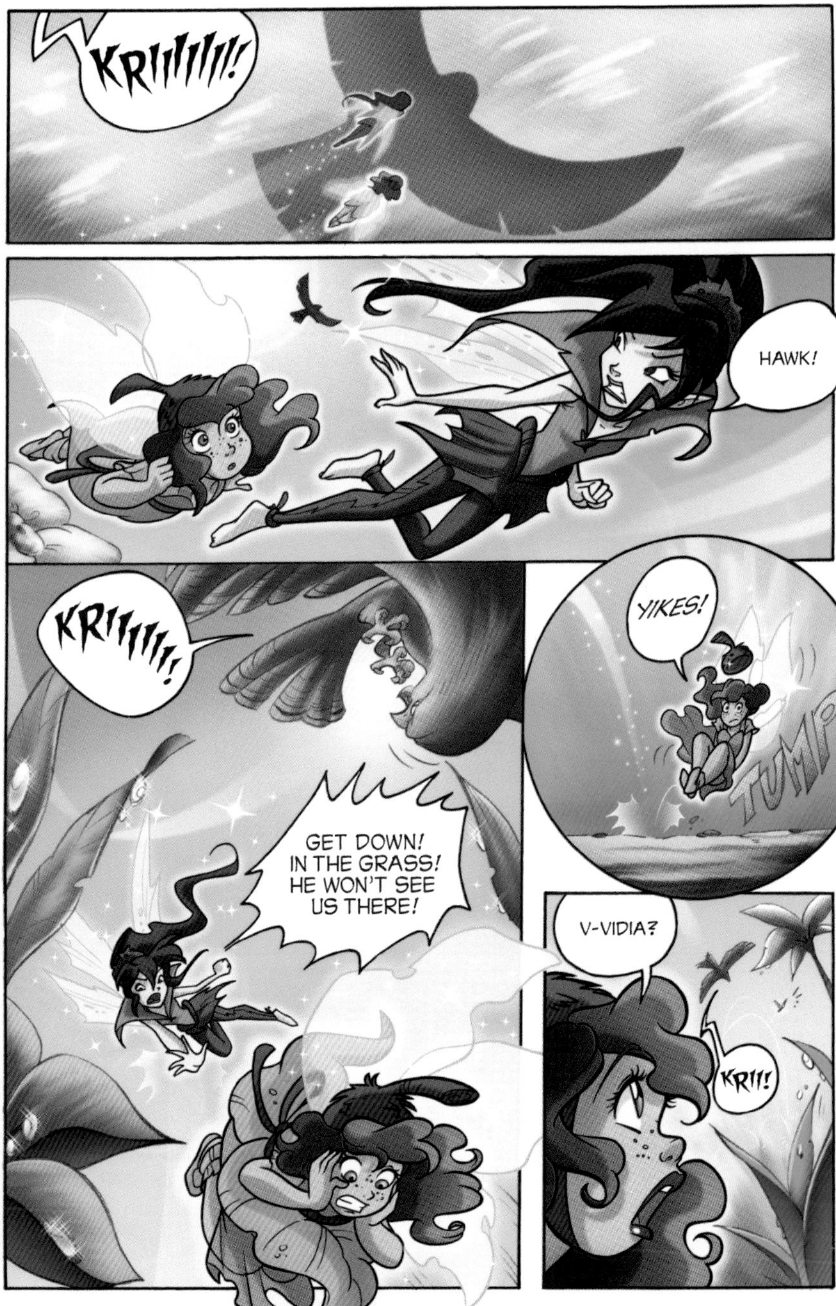

KRIIIIIII!
HAWK!
KRIIIIII!
YIKES!
TUMP
GET DOWN! IN THE GRASS! HE WON'T SEE US THERE!
V-VIDIA?
KRII!

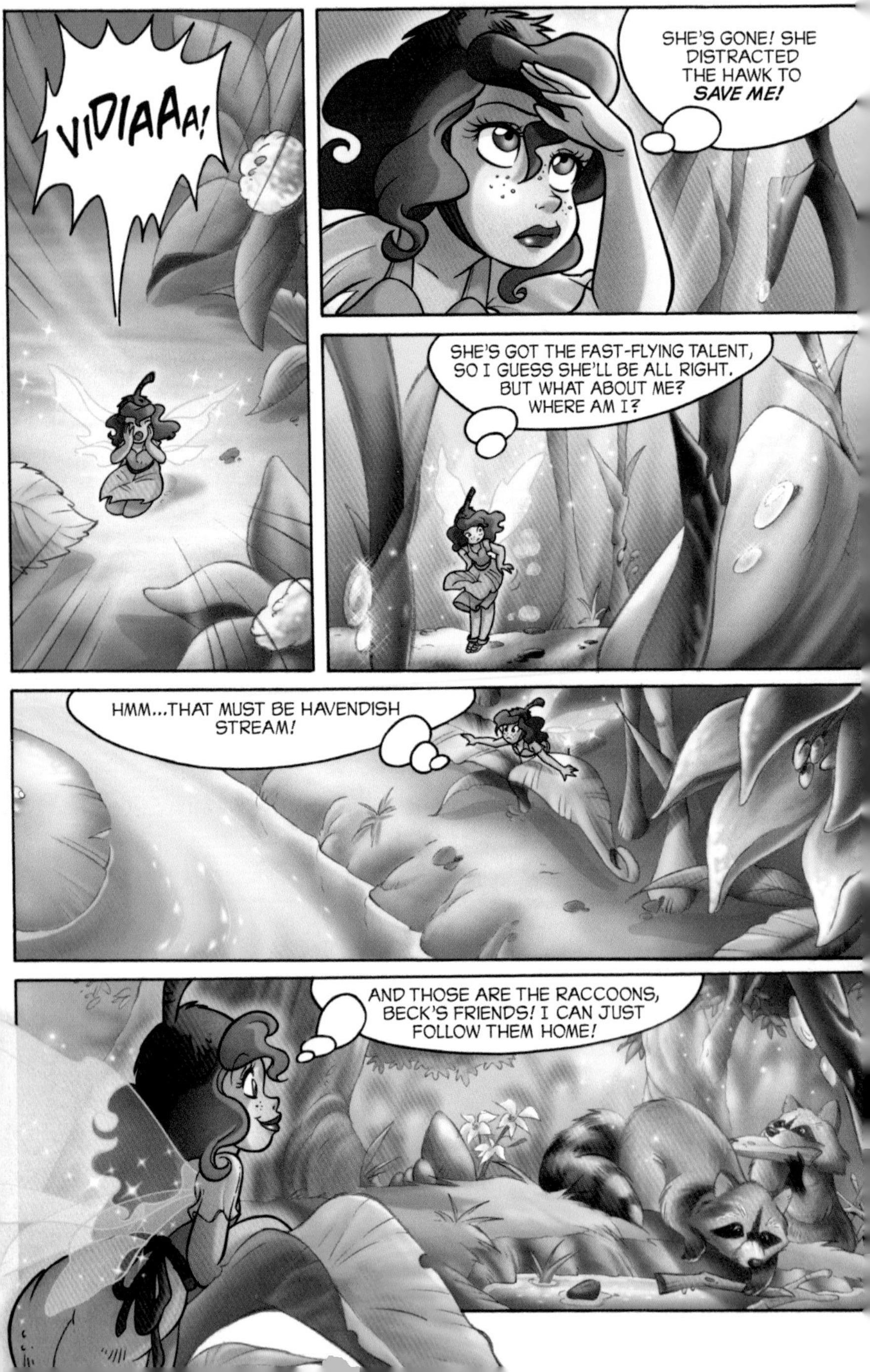
VIDIAAA!
SHE'S GONE! SHE DISTRACTED THE HAWK TO SAVE ME!
SHE'S GOT THE FAST-FLYING TALENT, SO I GUESS SHE'LL BE ALL RIGHT. BUT WHAT ABOUT ME? WHERE AM I?
HMM...THAT MUST BE HAVENDISH STREAM!
AND THOSE ARE THE RACCOONS, BECK'S FRIENDS! I CAN JUST FOLLOW THEM HOME!

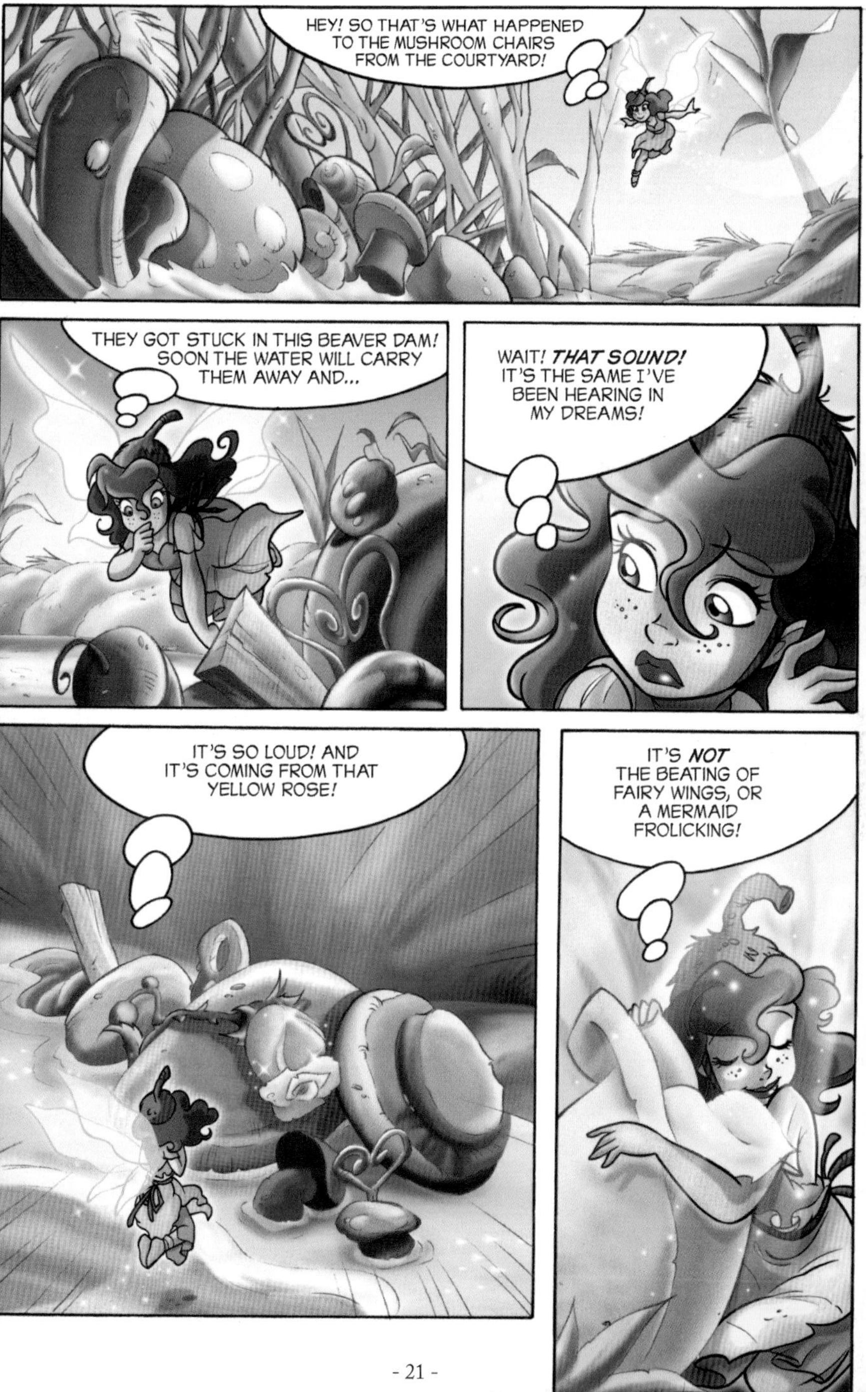
HEY! SO THAT'S WHAT HAPPENED TO THE MUSHROOM CHAIRS FROM THE COURTYARD!
THEY GOT STUCK IN THIS BEAVER DAM! SOON THE WATER WILL CARRY THEM AWAY AND...
WAIT! THAT SOUND! IT'S THE SAME I'VE BEEN HEARING IN MY DREAMS!
IT'S SO LOUD! AND IT'S COMING FROM THAT YELLOW ROSE!
IT'S NOT THE BEATING OF FAIRY WINGS, OR A MERMAID FROLICKING!

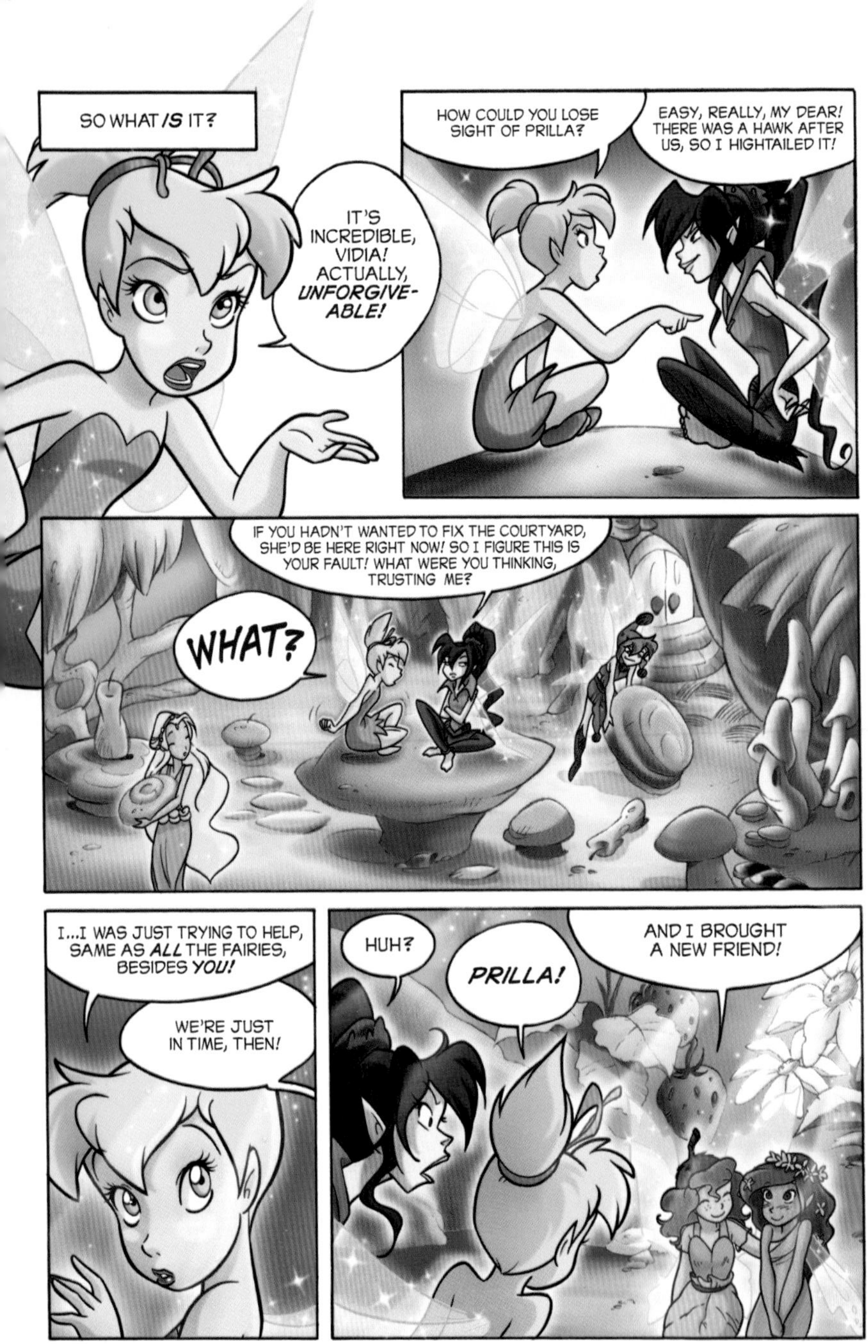
SO WHAT *IS* IT?
IT'S INCREDIBLE, VIDIA! ACTUALLY, ***UNFORGIVE-ABLE!***
HOW COULD YOU LOSE SIGHT OF PRILLA?
EASY, REALLY, MY DEAR! THERE WAS A HAWK AFTER US, SO I HIGHTAILED IT!
IF YOU HADN'T WANTED TO FIX THE COURTYARD, SHE'D BE HERE RIGHT NOW! SO I FIGURE THIS IS YOUR FAULT! WHAT WERE YOU THINKING, TRUSTING ME?
WHAT?
I...I WAS JUST TRYING TO HELP, SAME AS *ALL* THE FAIRIES, BESIDES *YOU!*
WE'RE JUST IN TIME, THEN!
HUH?
PRILLA!
AND I BROUGHT A NEW FRIEND!

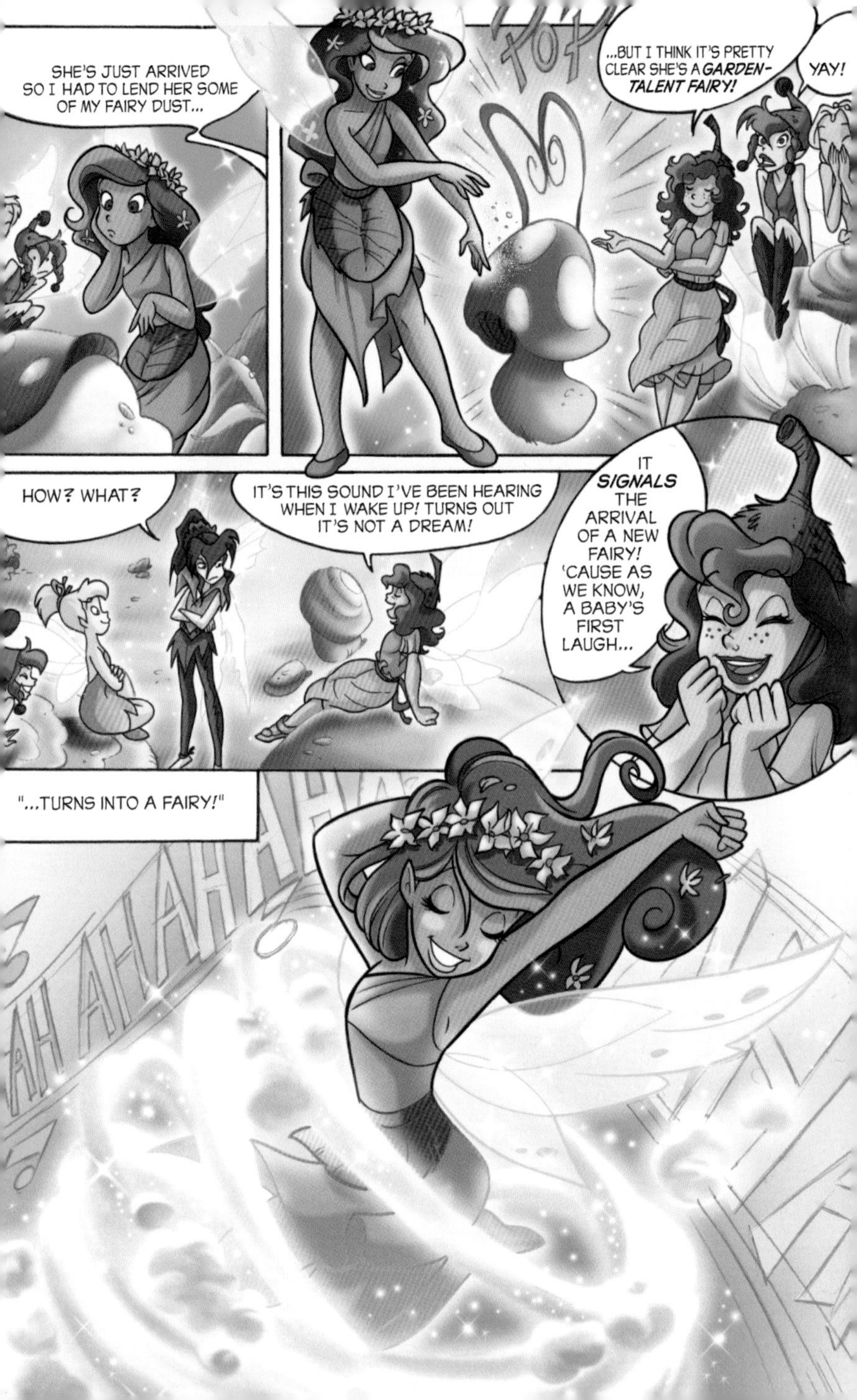

SHE'S JUST ARRIVED SO I HAD TO LEND HER SOME OF MY FAIRY DUST...
...BUT I THINK IT'S PRETTY CLEAR SHE'S A GARDEN-TALENT FAIRY!
YAY!
HOW? WHAT?
IT'S THIS SOUND I'VE BEEN HEARING WHEN I WAKE UP! TURNS OUT IT'S NOT A DREAM!
IT SIGNALS THE ARRIVAL OF A NEW FAIRY! 'CAUSE AS WE KNOW, A BABY'S FIRST LAUGH...
"...TURNS INTO A FAIRY!"
AH AHAHAH

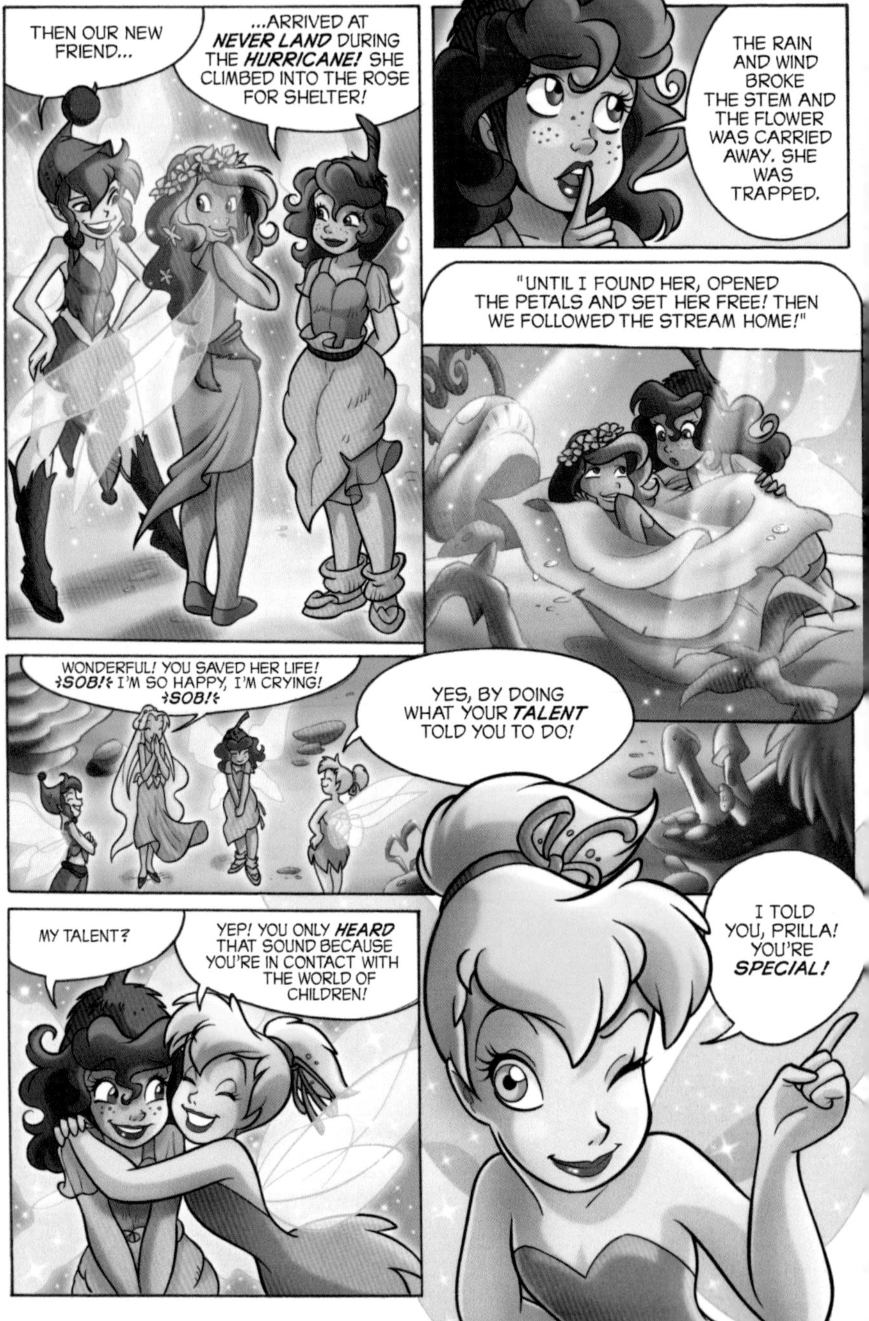
THEN OUR NEW FRIEND...
...ARRIVED AT NEVER LAND DURING THE HURRICANE! SHE CLIMBED INTO THE ROSE FOR SHELTER!
THE RAIN AND WIND BROKE THE STEM AND THE FLOWER WAS CARRIED AWAY. SHE WAS TRAPPED.
"UNTIL I FOUND HER, OPENED THE PETALS AND SET HER FREE! THEN WE FOLLOWED THE STREAM HOME!"
WONDERFUL! YOU SAVED HER LIFE! SOB! I'M SO HAPPY, I'M CRYING! SOB!
YES, BY DOING WHAT YOUR TALENT TOLD YOU TO DO!
MY TALENT?
YEP! YOU ONLY HEARD THAT SOUND BECAUSE YOU'RE IN CONTACT WITH THE WORLD OF CHILDREN!
I TOLD YOU, PRILLA! YOU'RE SPECIAL!

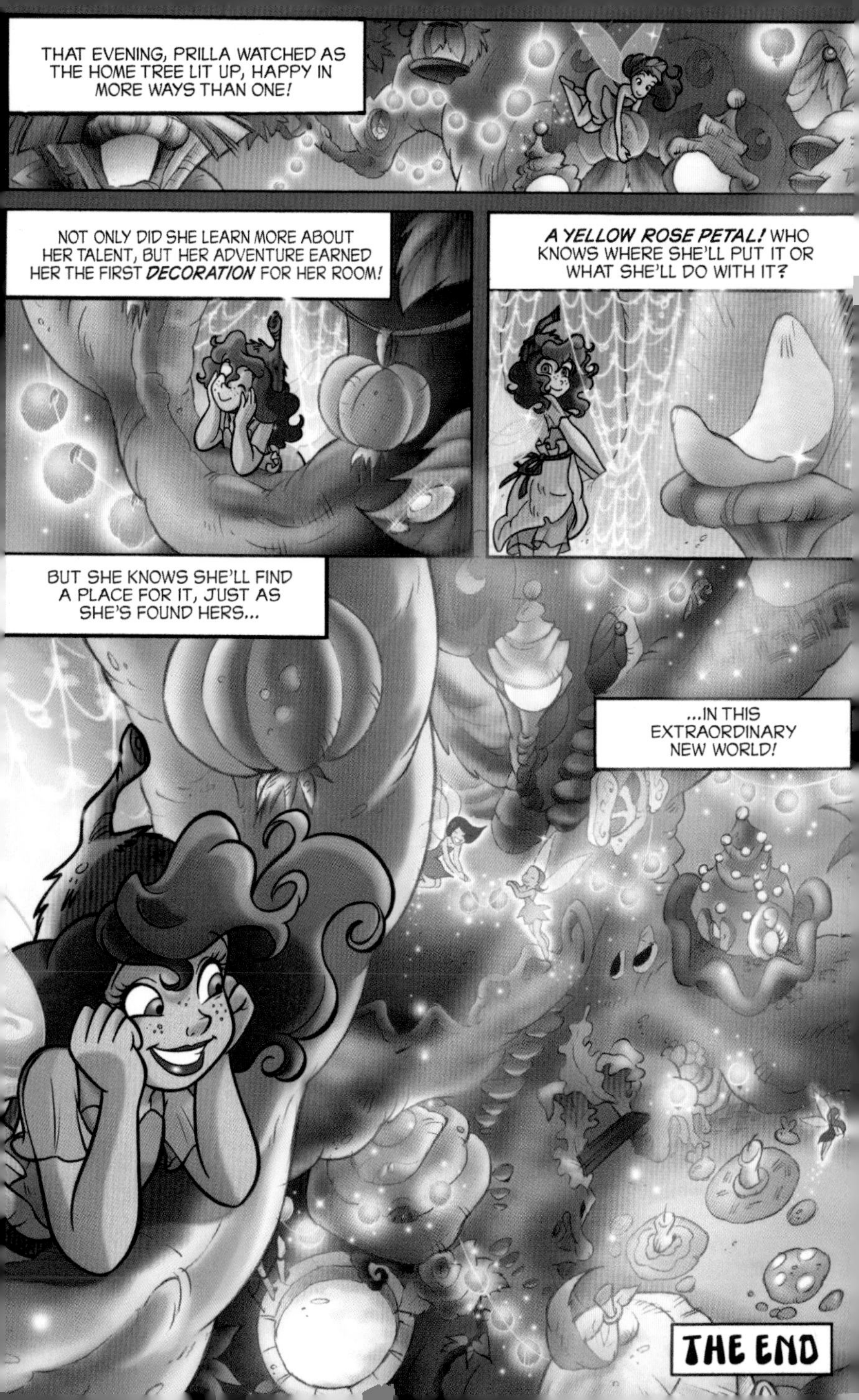
THAT EVENING, PRILLA WATCHED AS THE HOME TREE LIT UP, HAPPY IN MORE WAYS THAN ONE!
NOT ONLY DID SHE LEARN MORE ABOUT HER TALENT, BUT HER ADVENTURE EARNED HER THE FIRST *DECORATION* FOR HER ROOM!
A YELLOW ROSE PETAL! WHO KNOWS WHERE SHE'LL PUT IT OR WHAT SHE'LL DO WITH IT?
BUT SHE KNOWS SHE'LL FIND A PLACE FOR IT, JUST AS SHE'S FOUND HERS...
...IN THIS EXTRAORDINARY NEW WORLD!
THE END

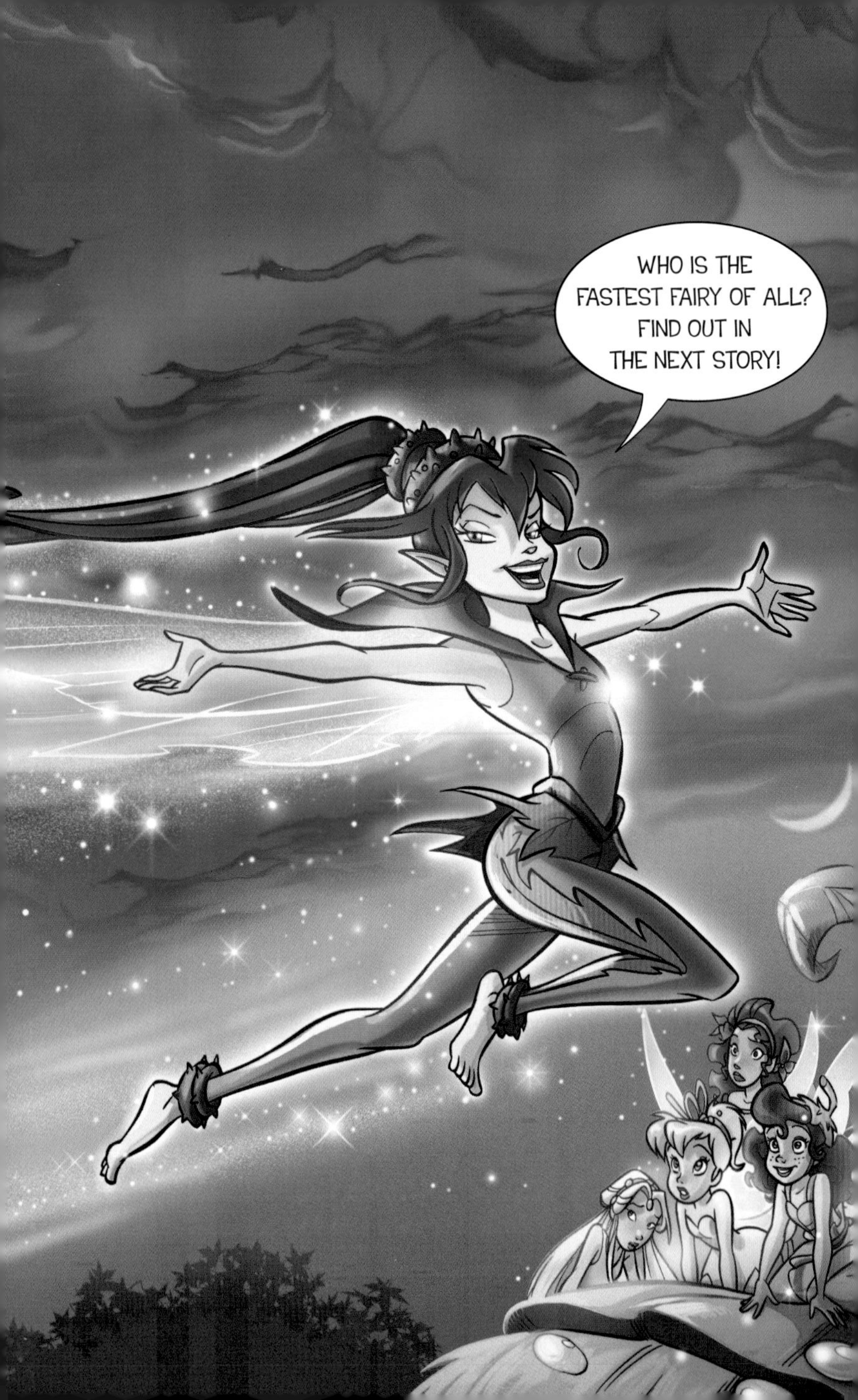
WHO IS THE FASTEST FAIRY OF ALL? FIND OUT IN THE NEXT STORY!

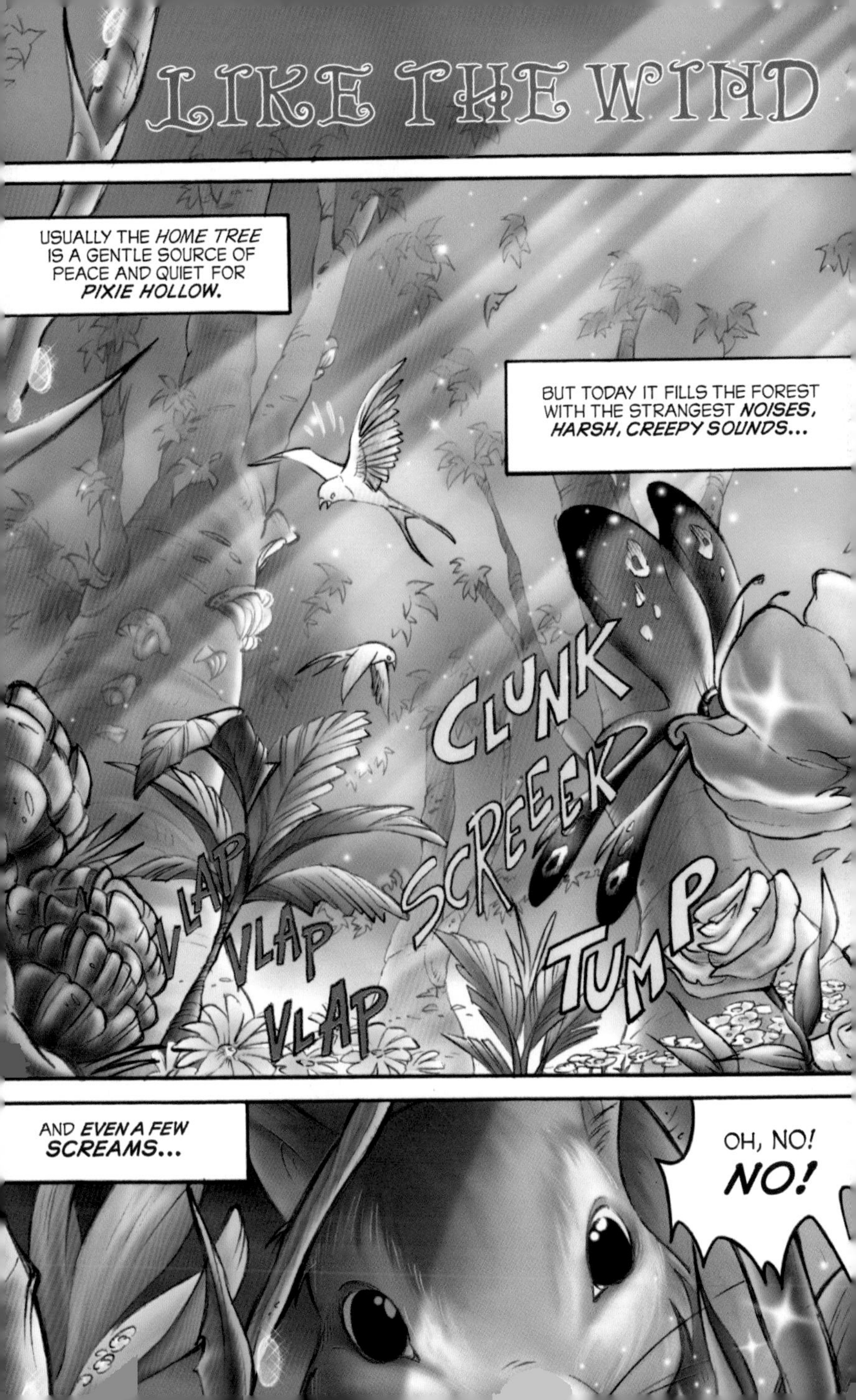
LIKE THE WIND
USUALLY THE *HOME TREE* IS A GENTLE SOURCE OF PEACE AND QUIET FOR *PIXIE HOLLOW.*
BUT TODAY IT FILLS THE FOREST WITH THE STRANGEST *NOISES, HARSH, CREEPY SOUNDS...*
VLAP
VLAP
VLAP
SCREEEK
CLUNK
TUMP
AND *EVEN A FEW SCREAMS...*
OH, NO! **NO!**

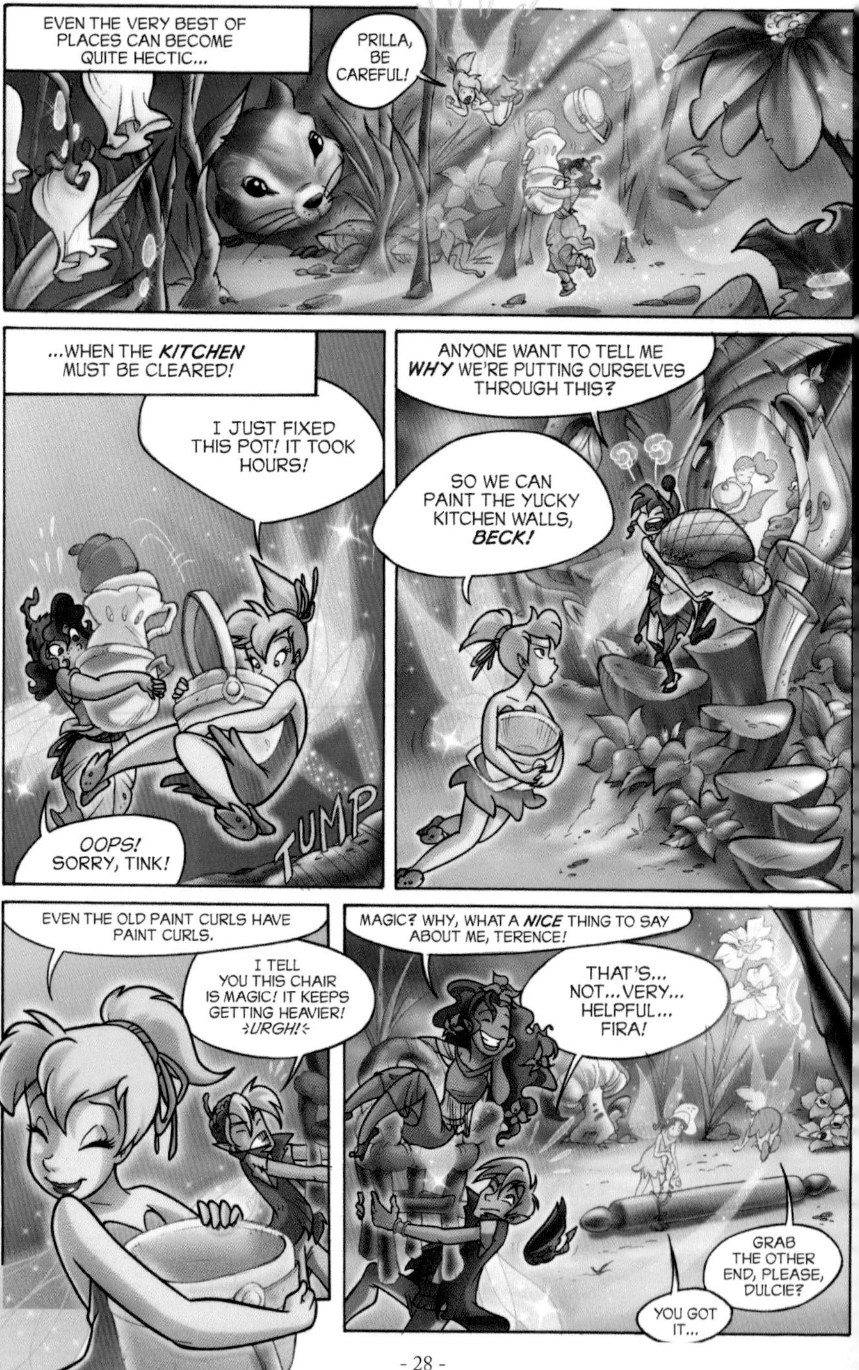
EVEN THE VERY BEST OF PLACES CAN BECOME QUITE HECTIC...
PRILLA, BE CAREFUL!
...WHEN THE KITCHEN MUST BE CLEARED!
I JUST FIXED THIS POT! IT TOOK HOURS!
OOPS! SORRY, TINK!
TUMP
ANYONE WANT TO TELL ME WHY WE'RE PUTTING OURSELVES THROUGH THIS?
SO WE CAN PAINT THE YUCKY KITCHEN WALLS, BECK!
EVEN THE OLD PAINT CURLS HAVE PAINT CURLS.
I TELL YOU THIS CHAIR IS MAGIC! IT KEEPS GETTING HEAVIER! URGH!
MAGIC? WHY, WHAT A NICE THING TO SAY ABOUT ME, TERENCE!
THAT'S... NOT...VERY... HELPFUL... FIRA!
GRAB THE OTHER END, PLEASE, DULCIE?
YOU GOT IT...

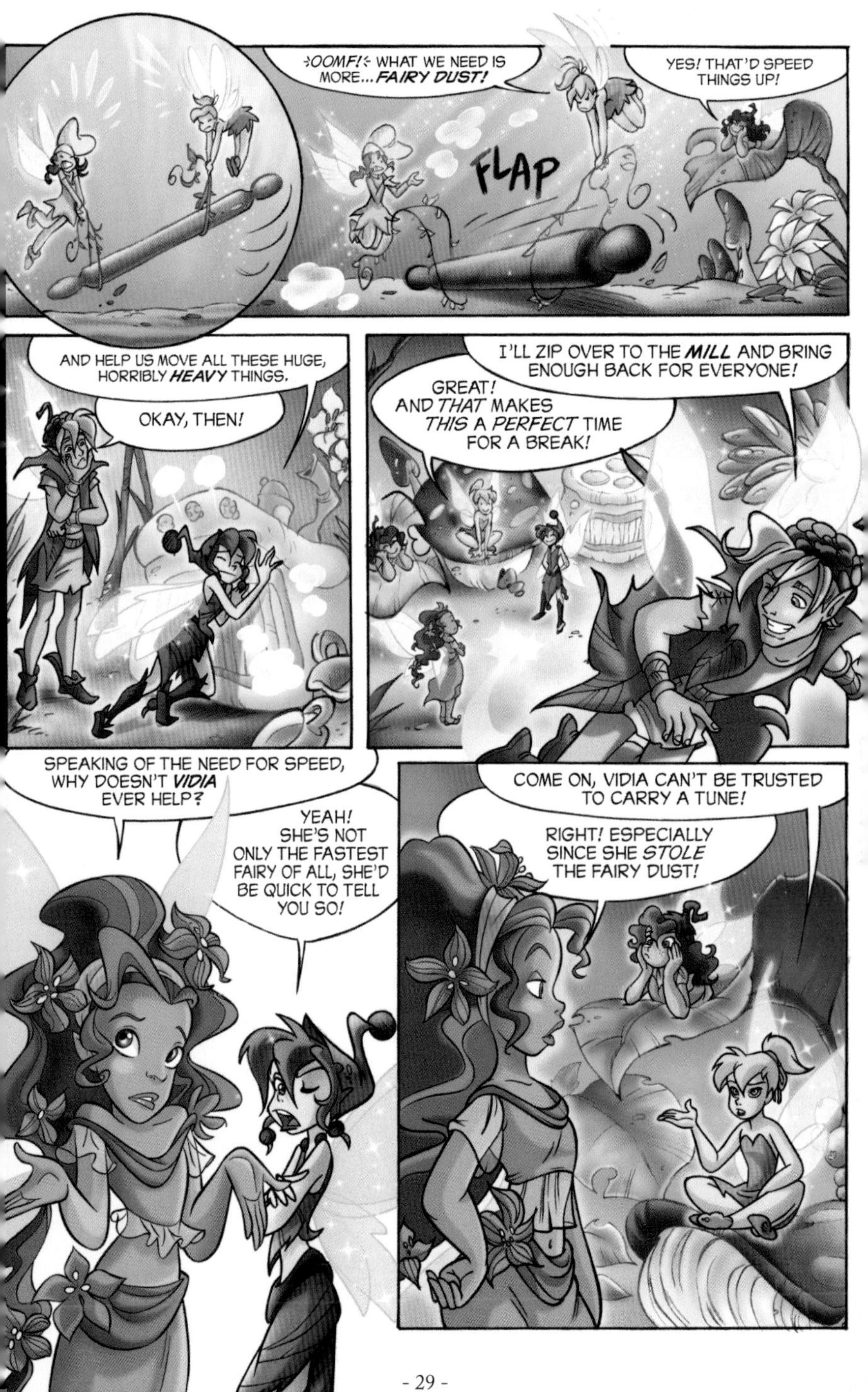

OOMF! WHAT WE NEED IS MORE... FAIRY DUST!
FLAP
YES! THAT'D SPEED THINGS UP!
AND HELP US MOVE ALL THESE HUGE, HORRIBLY HEAVY THINGS.
OKAY, THEN!
I'LL ZIP OVER TO THE MILL AND BRING ENOUGH BACK FOR EVERYONE!
GREAT! AND THAT MAKES THIS A PERFECT TIME FOR A BREAK!
SPEAKING OF THE NEED FOR SPEED, WHY DOESN'T VIDIA EVER HELP?
YEAH! SHE'S NOT ONLY THE FASTEST FAIRY OF ALL, SHE'D BE QUICK TO TELL YOU SO!
COME ON, VIDIA CAN'T BE TRUSTED TO CARRY A TUNE!
RIGHT! ESPECIALLY SINCE SHE STOLE THE FAIRY DUST!

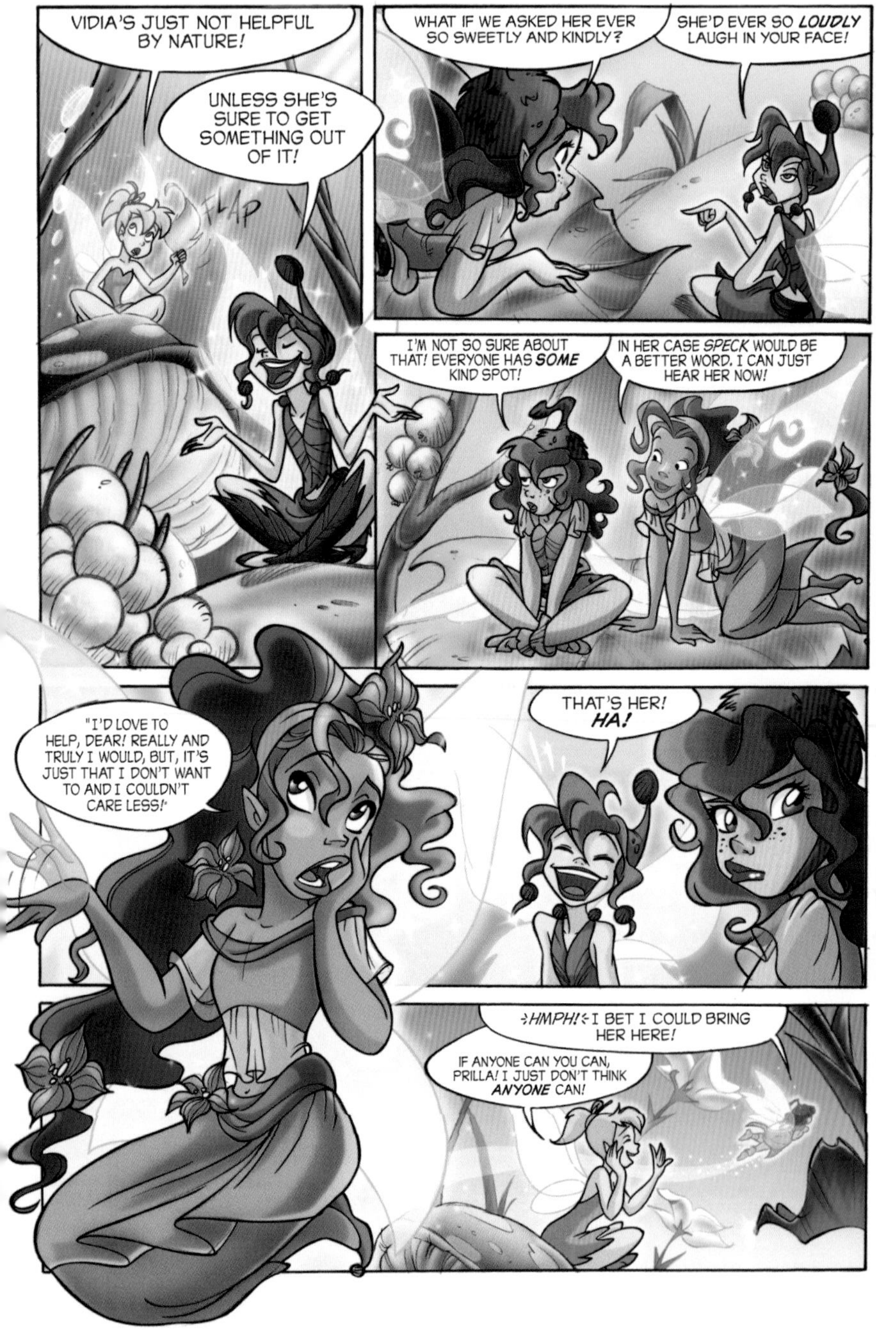
VIDIA'S JUST NOT HELPFUL BY NATURE!
UNLESS SHE'S SURE TO GET SOMETHING OUT OF IT!
FLAP
WHAT IF WE ASKED HER EVER SO SWEETLY AND KINDLY?
SHE'D EVER SO LOUDLY LAUGH IN YOUR FACE!
I'M NOT SO SURE ABOUT THAT! EVERYONE HAS SOME KIND SPOT!
IN HER CASE SPECK WOULD BE A BETTER WORD. I CAN JUST HEAR HER NOW!
"I'D LOVE TO HELP, DEAR! REALLY AND TRULY I WOULD, BUT, IT'S JUST THAT I DON'T WANT TO AND I COULDN'T CARE LESS!"
THAT'S HER! HA!
HMPH! I BET I COULD BRING HER HERE!
IF ANYONE CAN YOU CAN, PRILLA! I JUST DON'T THINK ANYONE CAN!

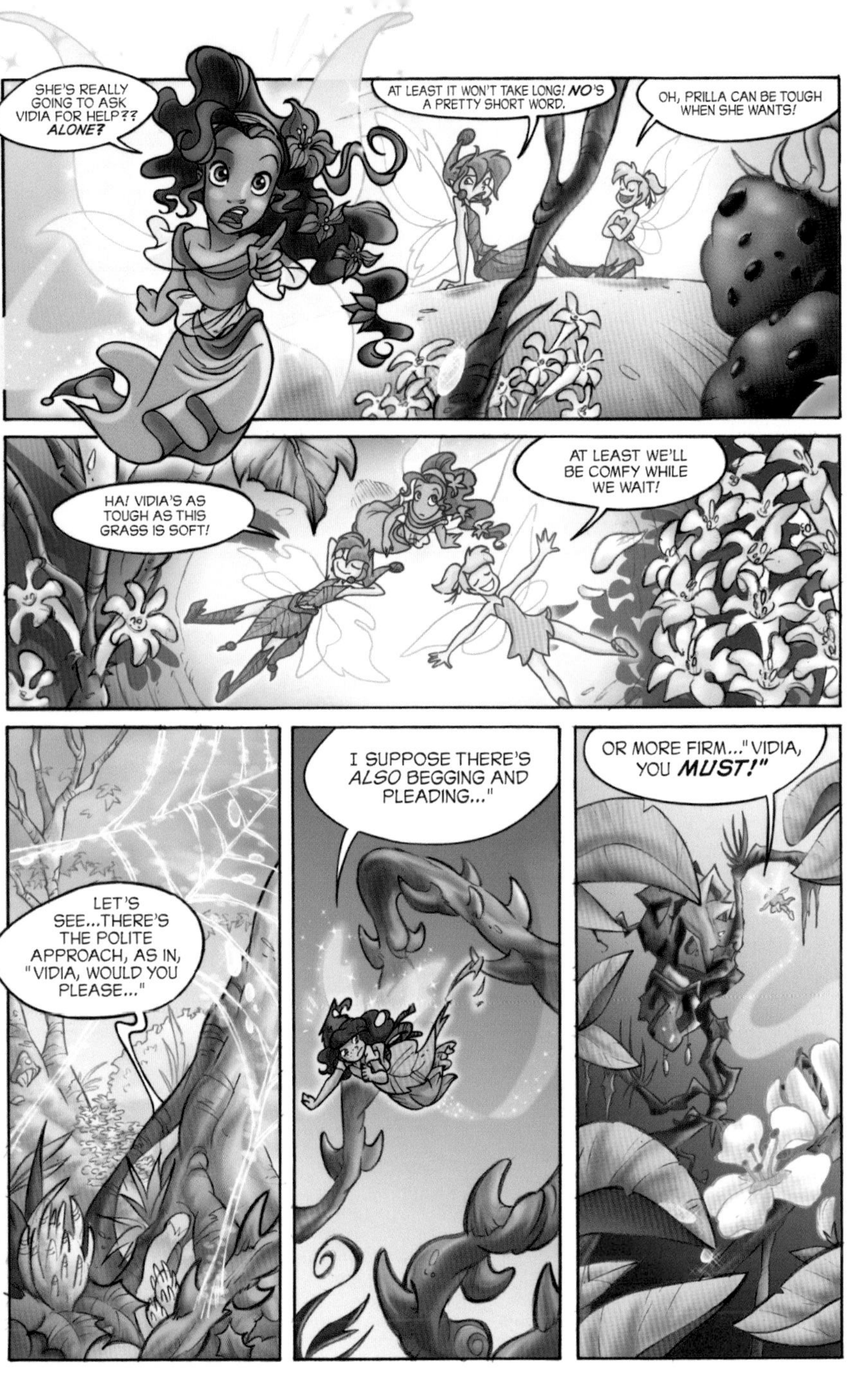
SHE'S REALLY GOING TO ASK VIDIA FOR HELP?? ALONE?
AT LEAST IT WON'T TAKE LONG! NO'S A PRETTY SHORT WORD.
OH, PRILLA CAN BE TOUGH WHEN SHE WANTS!
HA! VIDIA'S AS TOUGH AS THIS GRASS IS SOFT!
AT LEAST WE'LL BE COMFY WHILE WE WAIT!
LET'S SEE...THERE'S THE POLITE APPROACH, AS IN, "VIDIA, WOULD YOU PLEASE..."
I SUPPOSE THERE'S ALSO BEGGING AND PLEADING..."
OR MORE FIRM..."VIDIA, YOU MUST!"

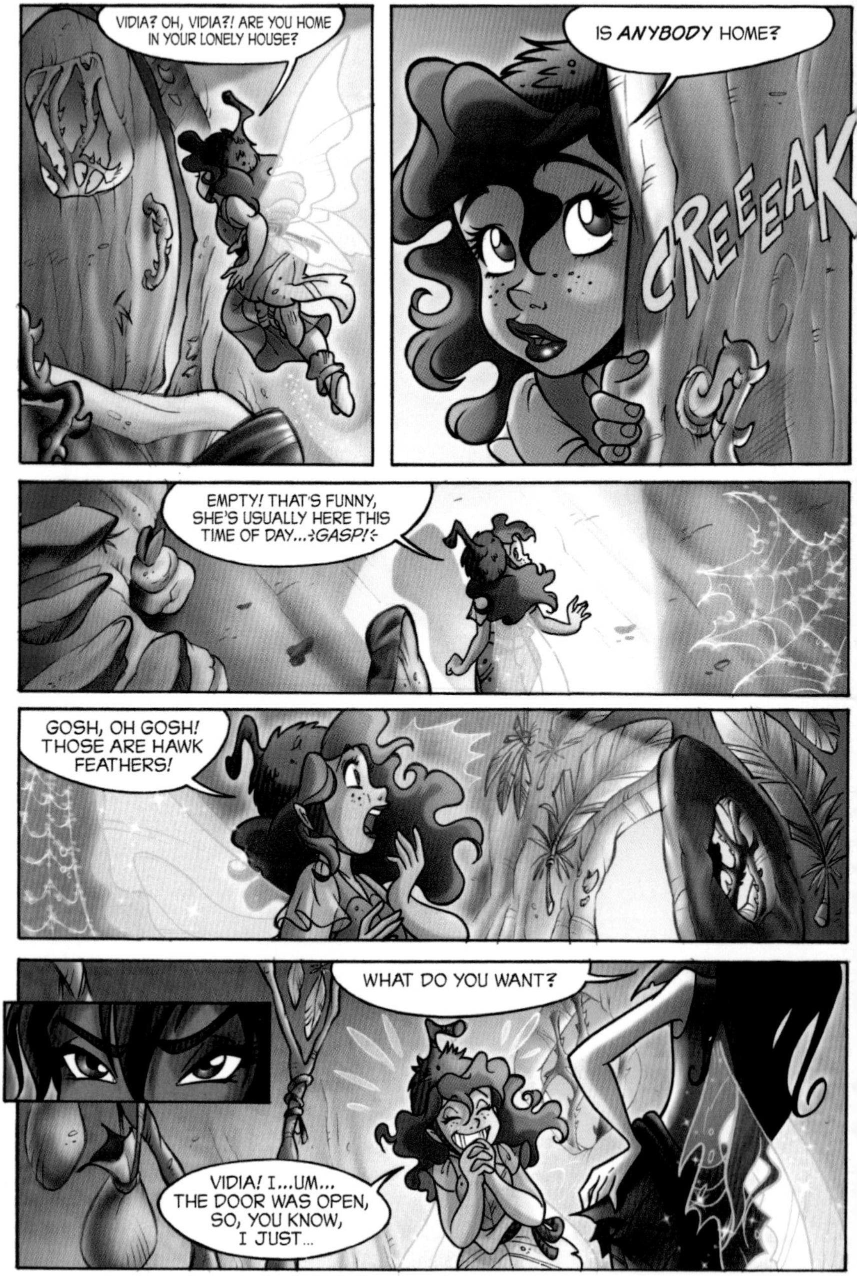
VIDIA? OH, VIDIA?! ARE YOU HOME IN YOUR LONELY HOUSE?
IS *ANYBODY* HOME?
CREEEAK
EMPTY! THAT'S FUNNY, SHE'S USUALLY HERE THIS TIME OF DAY... *GASP!*
GOSH, OH GOSH! THOSE ARE HAWK FEATHERS!
WHAT DO YOU WANT?
VIDIA! I...UM... THE DOOR WAS OPEN, SO, YOU KNOW, I JUST...

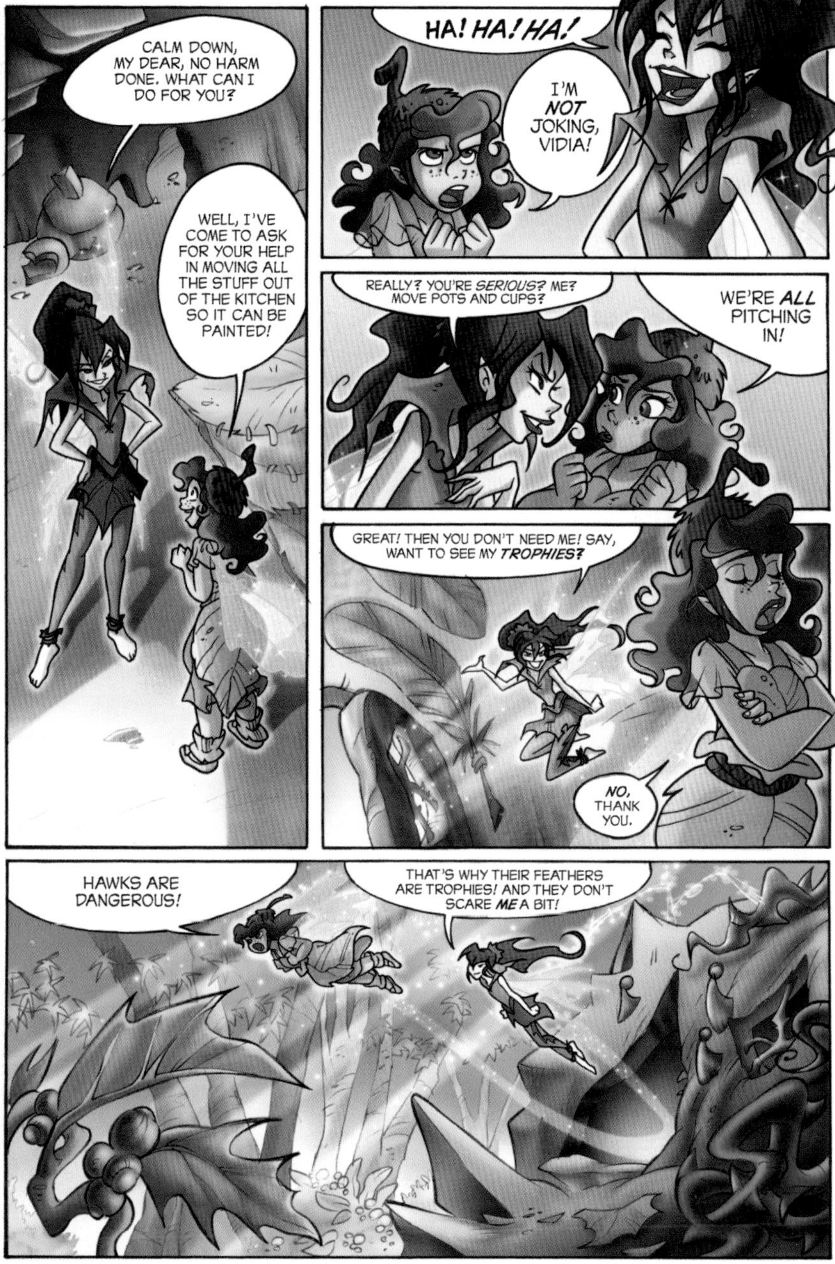
CALM DOWN, MY DEAR, NO HARM DONE. WHAT CAN I DO FOR YOU?
WELL, I'VE COME TO ASK FOR YOUR HELP IN MOVING ALL THE STUFF OUT OF THE KITCHEN SO IT CAN BE PAINTED!
HA! HA! HA!
I'M NOT JOKING, VIDIA!
REALLY? YOU'RE SERIOUS? ME? MOVE POTS AND CUPS?
WE'RE ALL PITCHING IN!
GREAT! THEN YOU DON'T NEED ME! SAY, WANT TO SEE MY TROPHIES?
NO, THANK YOU.
HAWKS ARE DANGEROUS!
THAT'S WHY THEIR FEATHERS ARE TROPHIES! AND THEY DON'T SCARE ME A BIT!

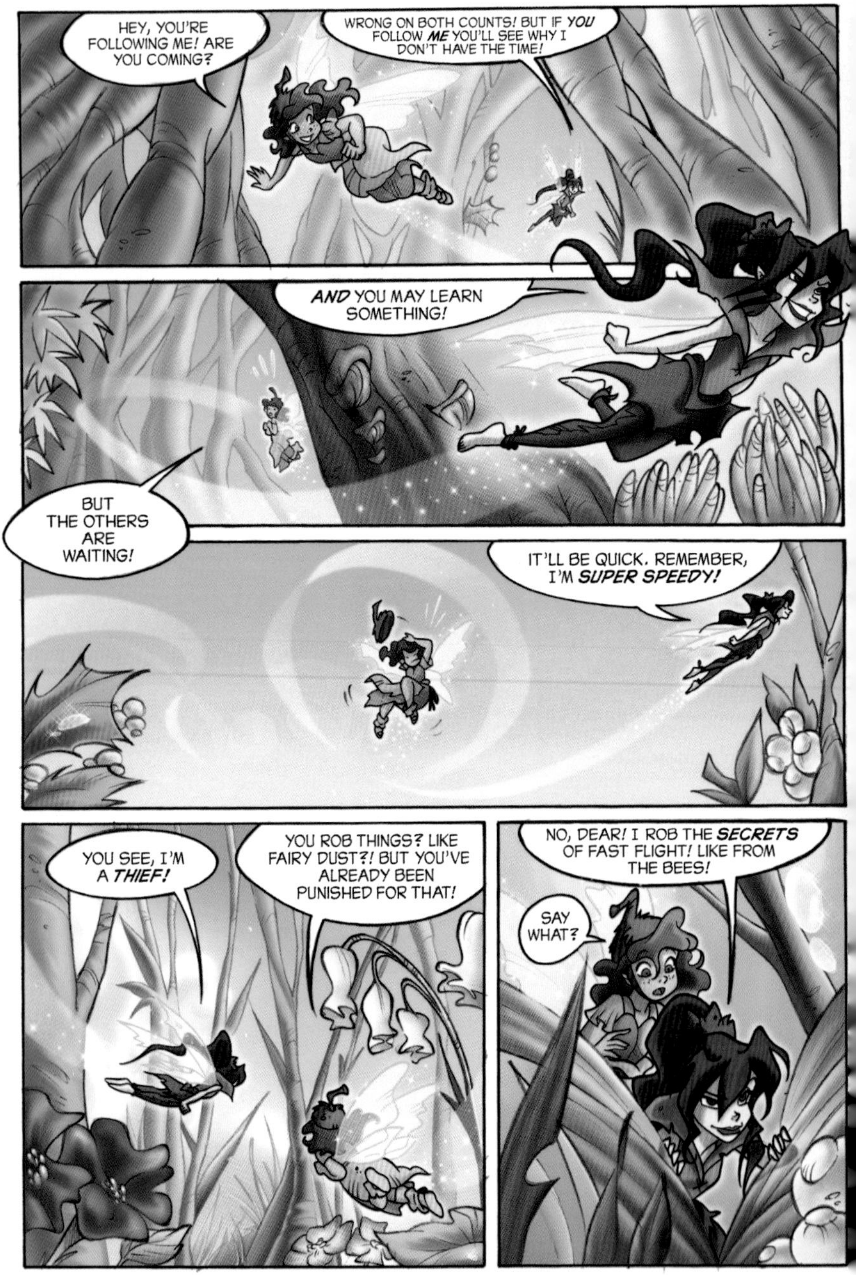

HEY, YOU'RE FOLLOWING ME! ARE YOU COMING?
WRONG ON BOTH COUNTS! BUT IF YOU FOLLOW ME YOU'LL SEE WHY I DON'T HAVE THE TIME!
AND YOU MAY LEARN SOMETHING!
BUT THE OTHERS ARE WAITING!
IT'LL BE QUICK. REMEMBER, I'M SUPER SPEEDY!
YOU SEE, I'M A THIEF!
YOU ROB THINGS? LIKE FAIRY DUST?! BUT YOU'VE ALREADY BEEN PUNISHED FOR THAT!
NO, DEAR! I ROB THE SECRETS OF FAST FLIGHT! LIKE FROM THE BEES!
SAY WHAT?

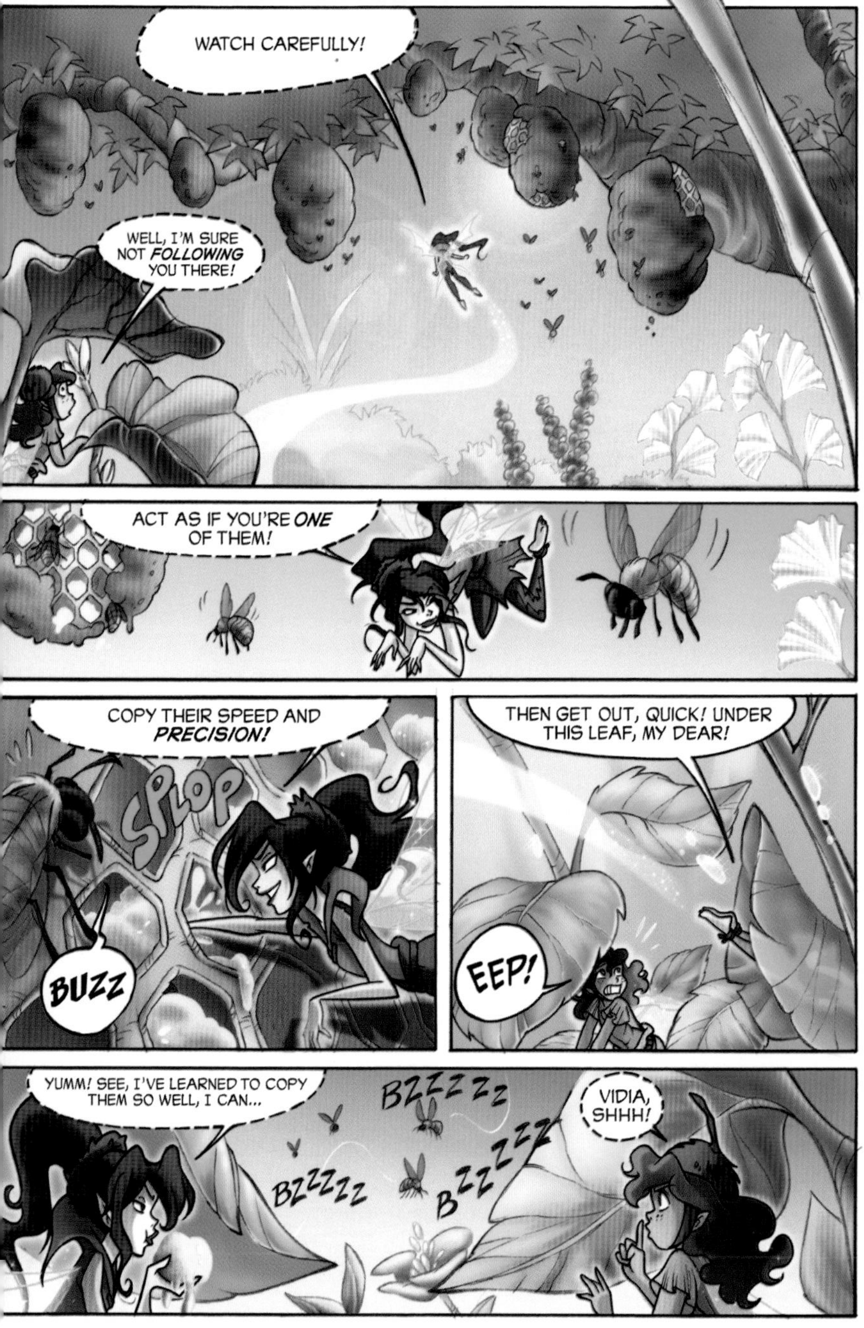
WATCH CAREFULLY!
WELL, I'M SURE NOT *FOLLOWING* YOU THERE!
ACT AS IF YOU'RE *ONE* OF THEM!
COPY THEIR SPEED AND *PRECISION!*
SPLOP
BUZZ
THEN GET OUT, QUICK! UNDER THIS LEAF, MY DEAR!
EEP!
YUMM! SEE, I'VE LEARNED TO COPY THEM SO WELL, I CAN...
BZZZZZ
VIDIA, SHHH!
BZZZZZ
BZZZZZZ

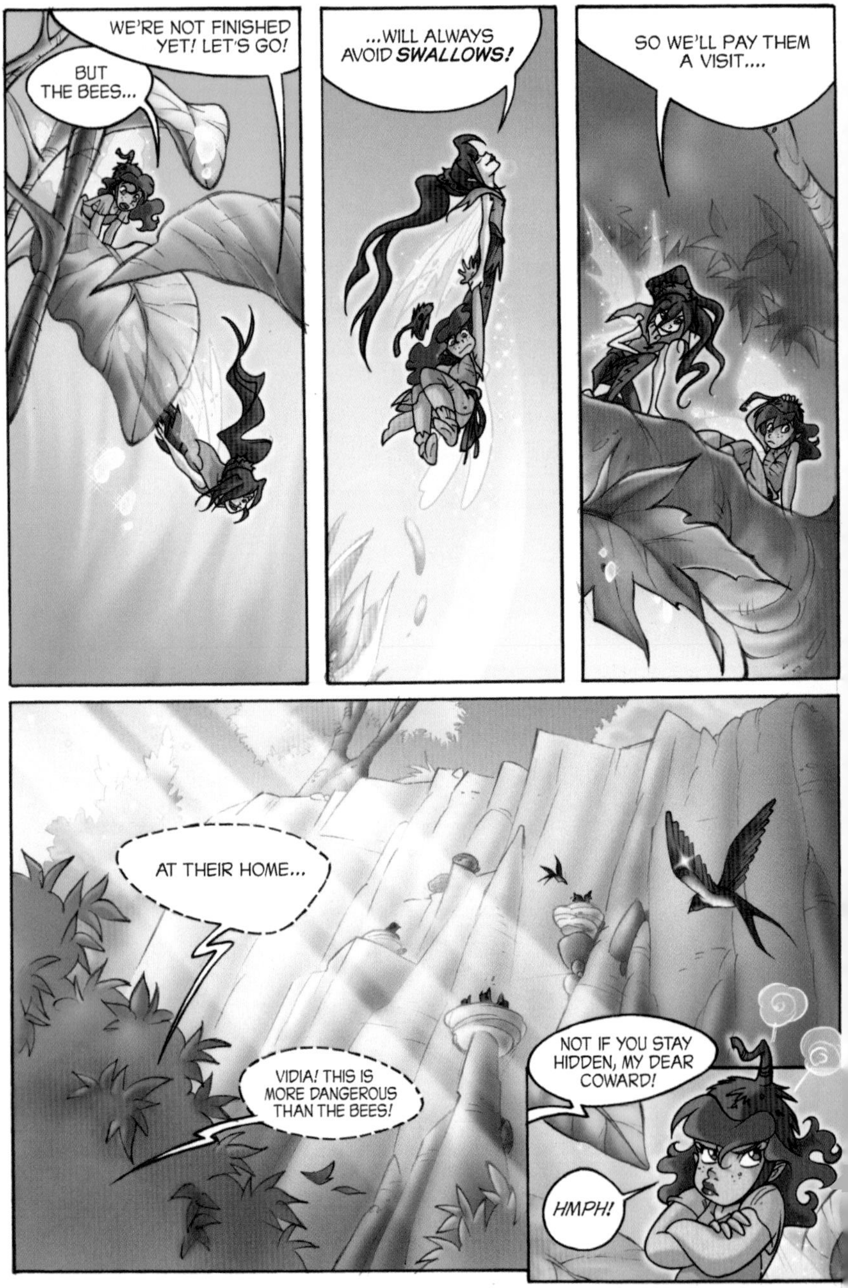
WE'RE NOT FINISHED YET! LET'S GO!
BUT THE BEES...
...WILL ALWAYS AVOID SWALLOWS!
SO WE'LL PAY THEM A VISIT....
AT THEIR HOME...
VIDIA! THIS IS MORE DANGEROUS THAN THE BEES!
NOT IF YOU STAY HIDDEN, MY DEAR COWARD!
HMPH!

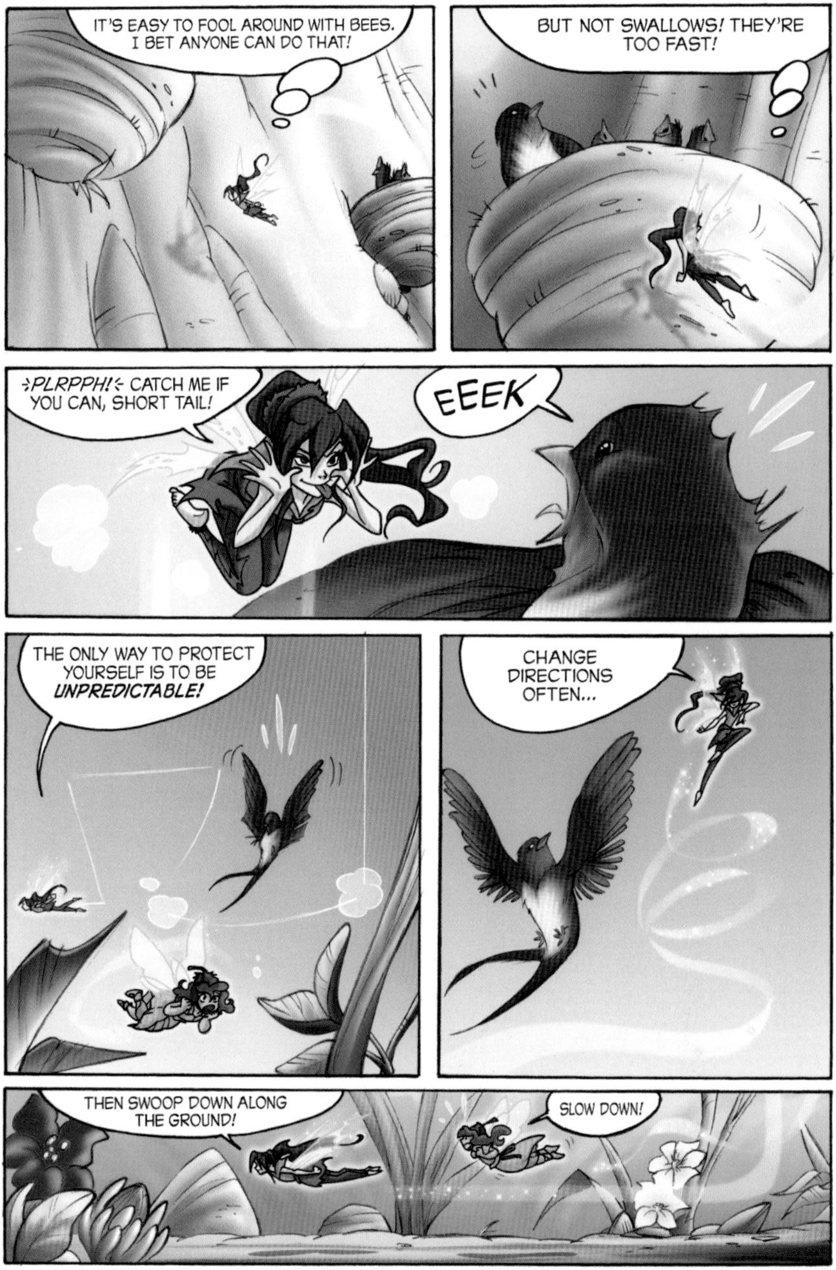
IT'S EASY TO FOOL AROUND WITH BEES. I BET ANYONE CAN DO THAT!
BUT NOT SWALLOWS! THEY'RE TOO FAST!
PLRPPH! CATCH ME IF YOU CAN, SHORT TAIL!
EEEK
THE ONLY WAY TO PROTECT YOURSELF IS TO BE UNPREDICTABLE!
CHANGE DIRECTIONS OFTEN...
THEN SWOOP DOWN ALONG THE GROUND!
SLOW DOWN!

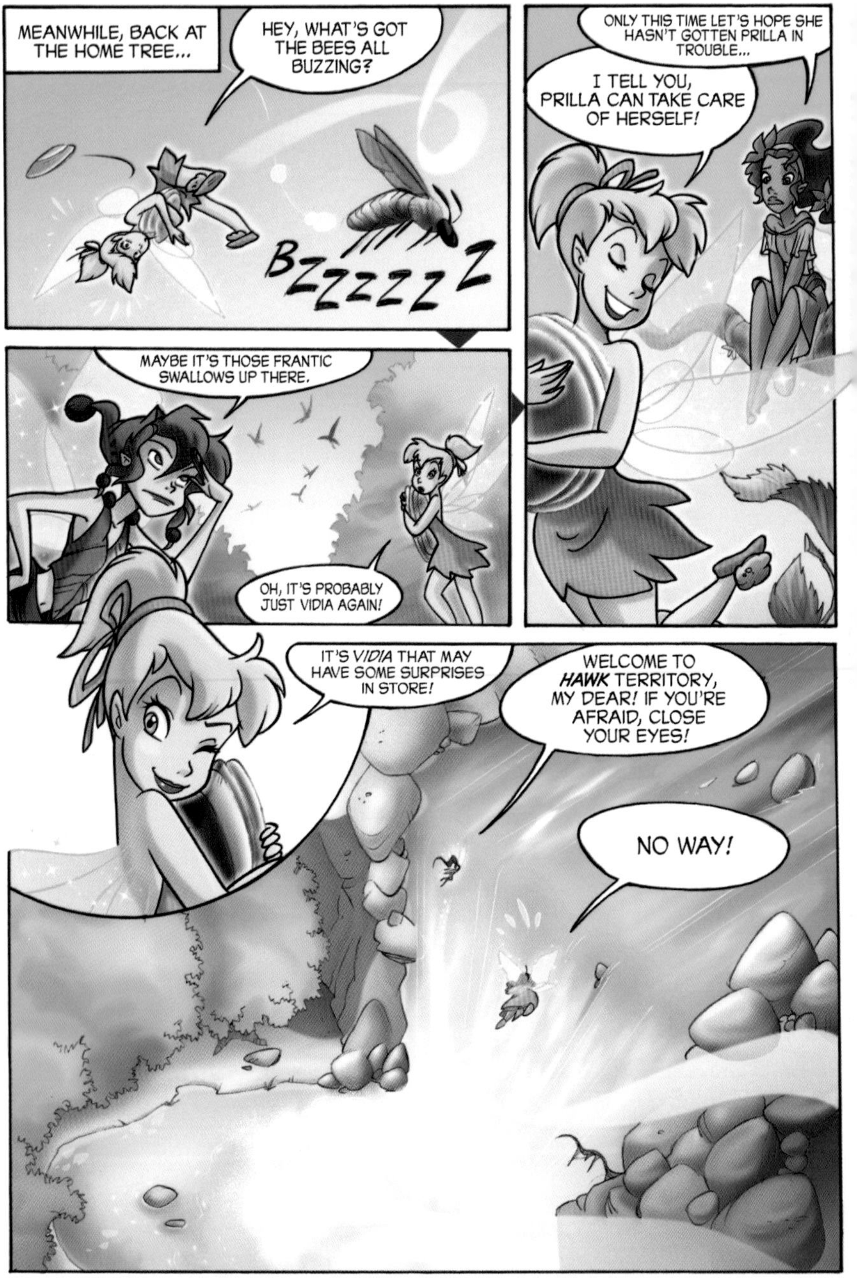
MEANWHILE, BACK AT THE HOME TREE...
HEY, WHAT'S GOT THE BEES ALL BUZZING?
BZZZZZZZ
ONLY THIS TIME LET'S HOPE SHE HASN'T GOTTEN PRILLA IN TROUBLE...
I TELL YOU, PRILLA CAN TAKE CARE OF HERSELF!
MAYBE IT'S THOSE FRANTIC SWALLOWS UP THERE.
OH, IT'S PROBABLY JUST VIDIA AGAIN!
IT'S VIDIA THAT MAY HAVE SOME SURPRISES IN STORE!
WELCOME TO HAWK TERRITORY, MY DEAR! IF YOU'RE AFRAID, CLOSE YOUR EYES!
NO WAY!

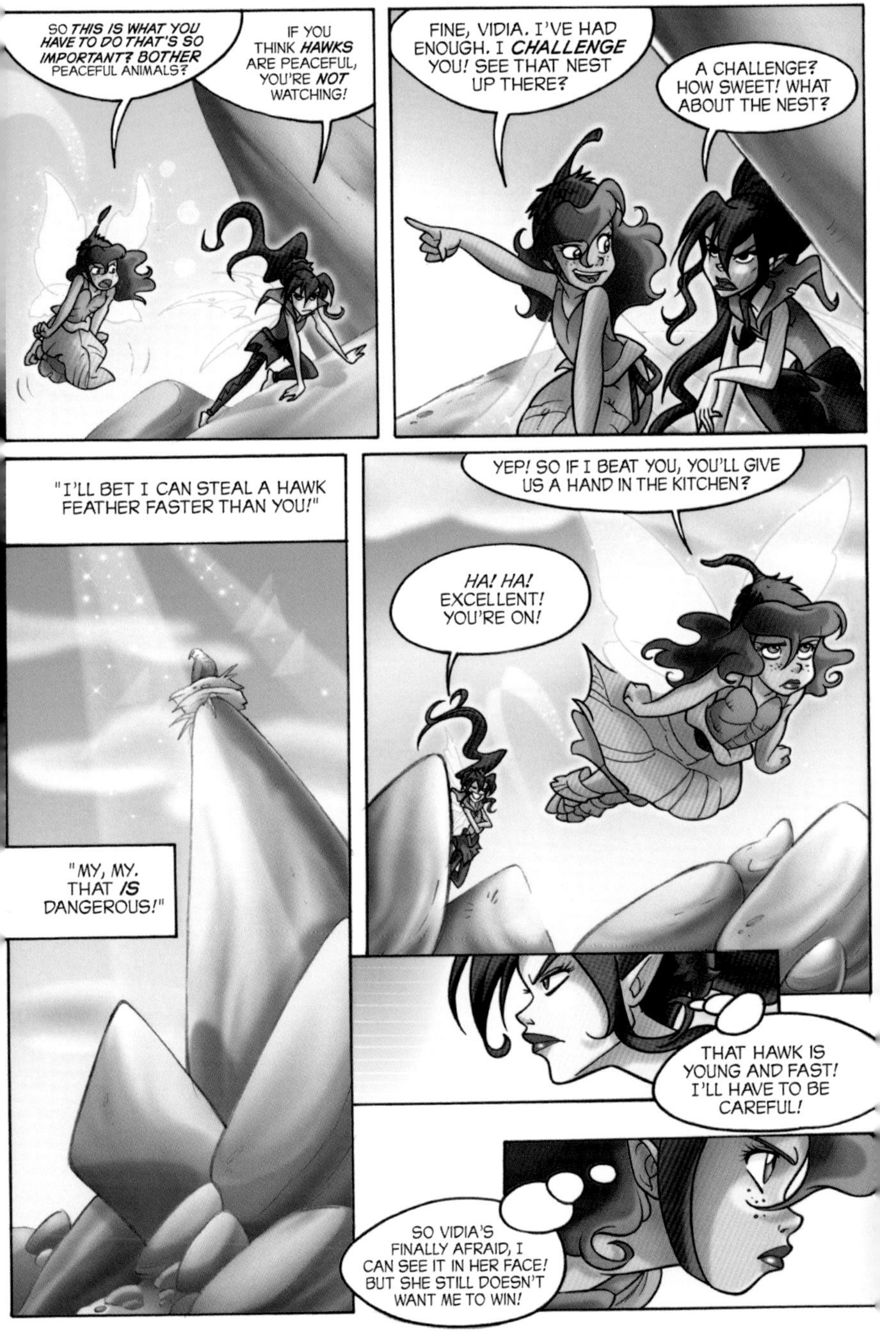
SO THIS IS WHAT YOU HAVE TO DO THAT'S SO IMPORTANT? BOTHER PEACEFUL ANIMALS?
IF YOU THINK HAWKS ARE PEACEFUL, YOU'RE NOT WATCHING!
FINE, VIDIA. I'VE HAD ENOUGH. I CHALLENGE YOU! SEE THAT NEST UP THERE?
A CHALLENGE? HOW SWEET! WHAT ABOUT THE NEST?
"I'LL BET I CAN STEAL A HAWK FEATHER FASTER THAN YOU!"
"MY, MY. THAT IS DANGEROUS!"
YEP! SO IF I BEAT YOU, YOU'LL GIVE US A HAND IN THE KITCHEN?
HA! HA! EXCELLENT! YOU'RE ON!
THAT HAWK IS YOUNG AND FAST! I'LL HAVE TO BE CAREFUL!
SO VIDIA'S FINALLY AFRAID, I CAN SEE IT IN HER FACE! BUT SHE STILL DOESN'T WANT ME TO WIN!

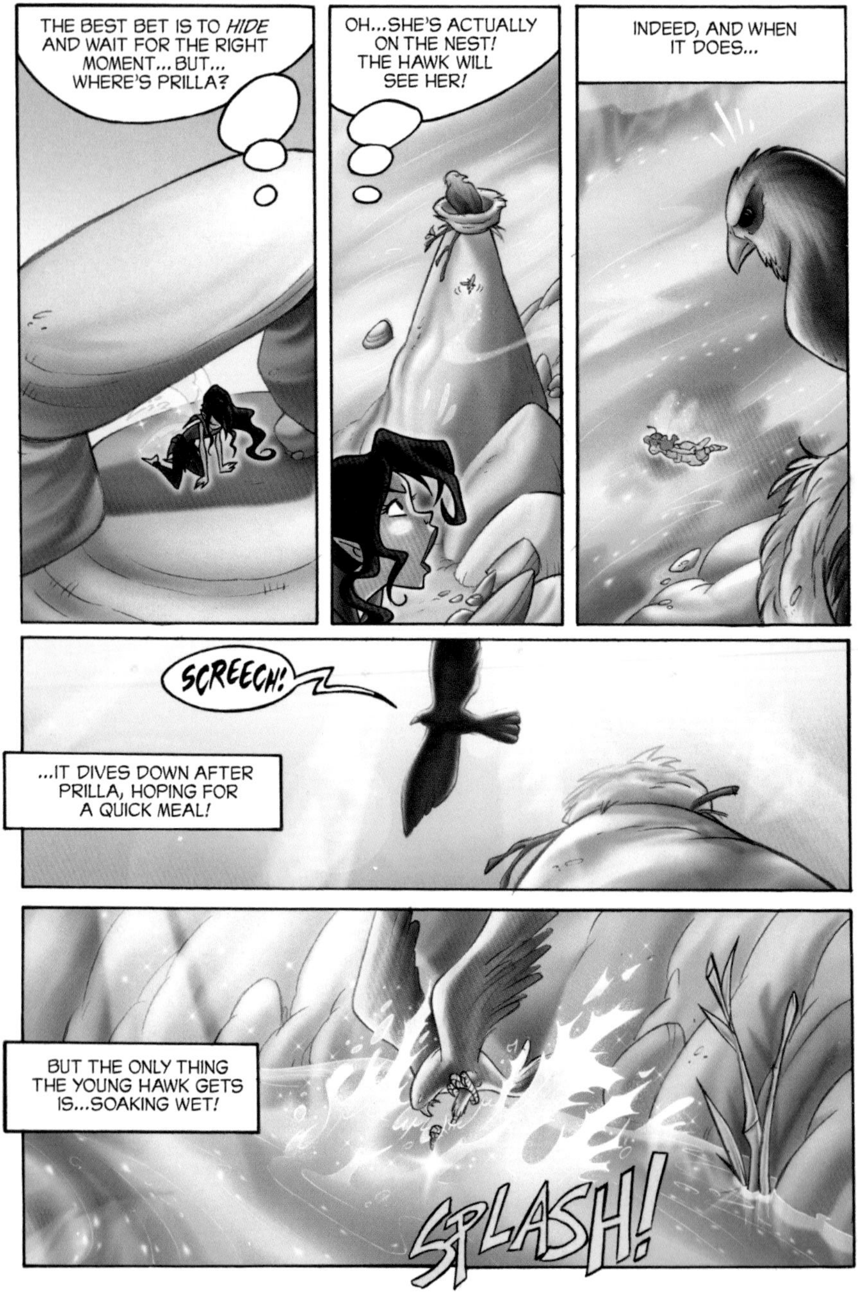
THE BEST BET IS TO *HIDE* AND WAIT FOR THE RIGHT MOMENT... BUT... WHERE'S PRILLA?
OH...SHE'S ACTUALLY ON THE NEST! THE HAWK WILL SEE HER!
INDEED, AND WHEN IT DOES...
SCREECH!
...IT DIVES DOWN AFTER PRILLA, HOPING FOR A QUICK MEAL!
BUT THE ONLY THING THE YOUNG HAWK GETS IS...SOAKING WET!
SPLASH!

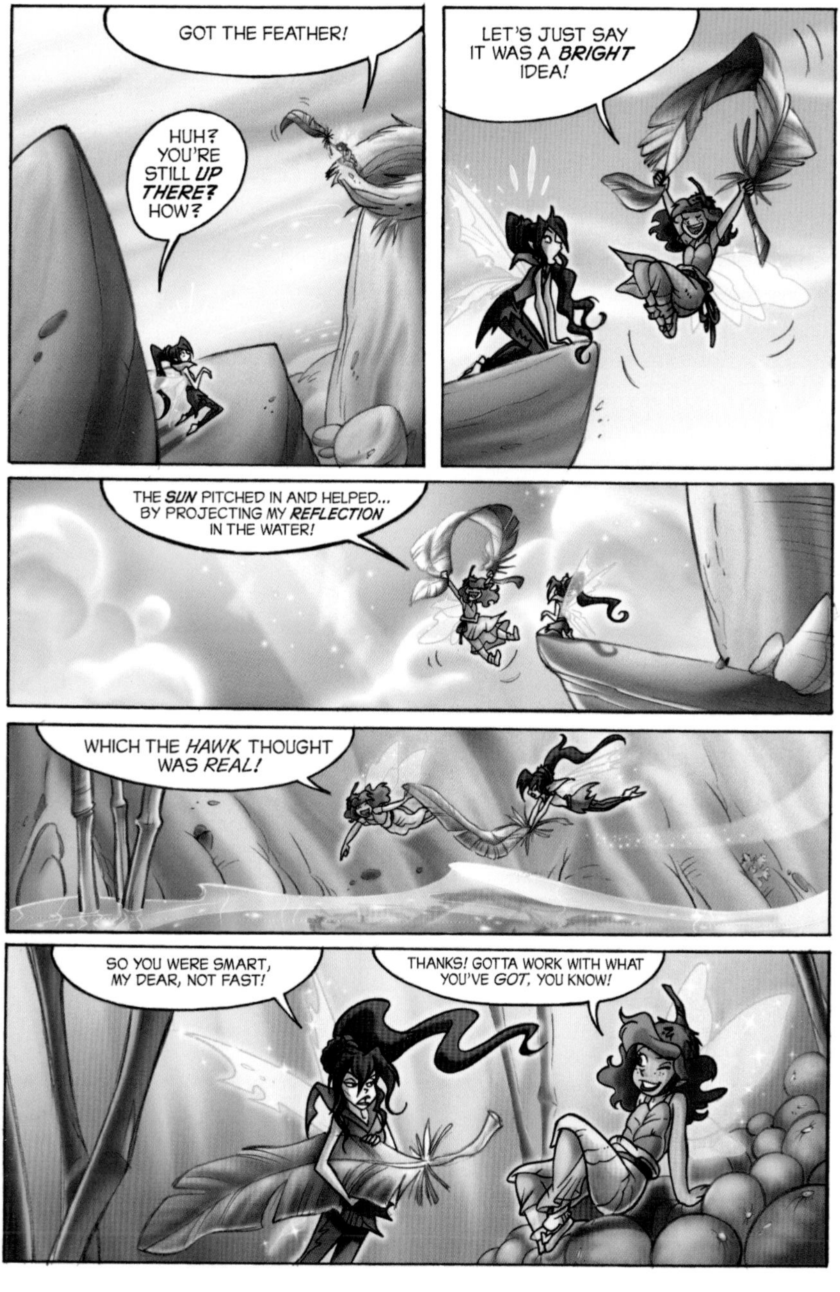
GOT THE FEATHER!
HUH? YOU'RE STILL UP THERE? HOW?
LET'S JUST SAY IT WAS A BRIGHT IDEA!
THE SUN PITCHED IN AND HELPED... BY PROJECTING MY REFLECTION IN THE WATER!
WHICH THE HAWK THOUGHT WAS REAL!
SO YOU WERE SMART, MY DEAR, NOT FAST!
THANKS! GOTTA WORK WITH WHAT YOU'VE GOT, YOU KNOW!

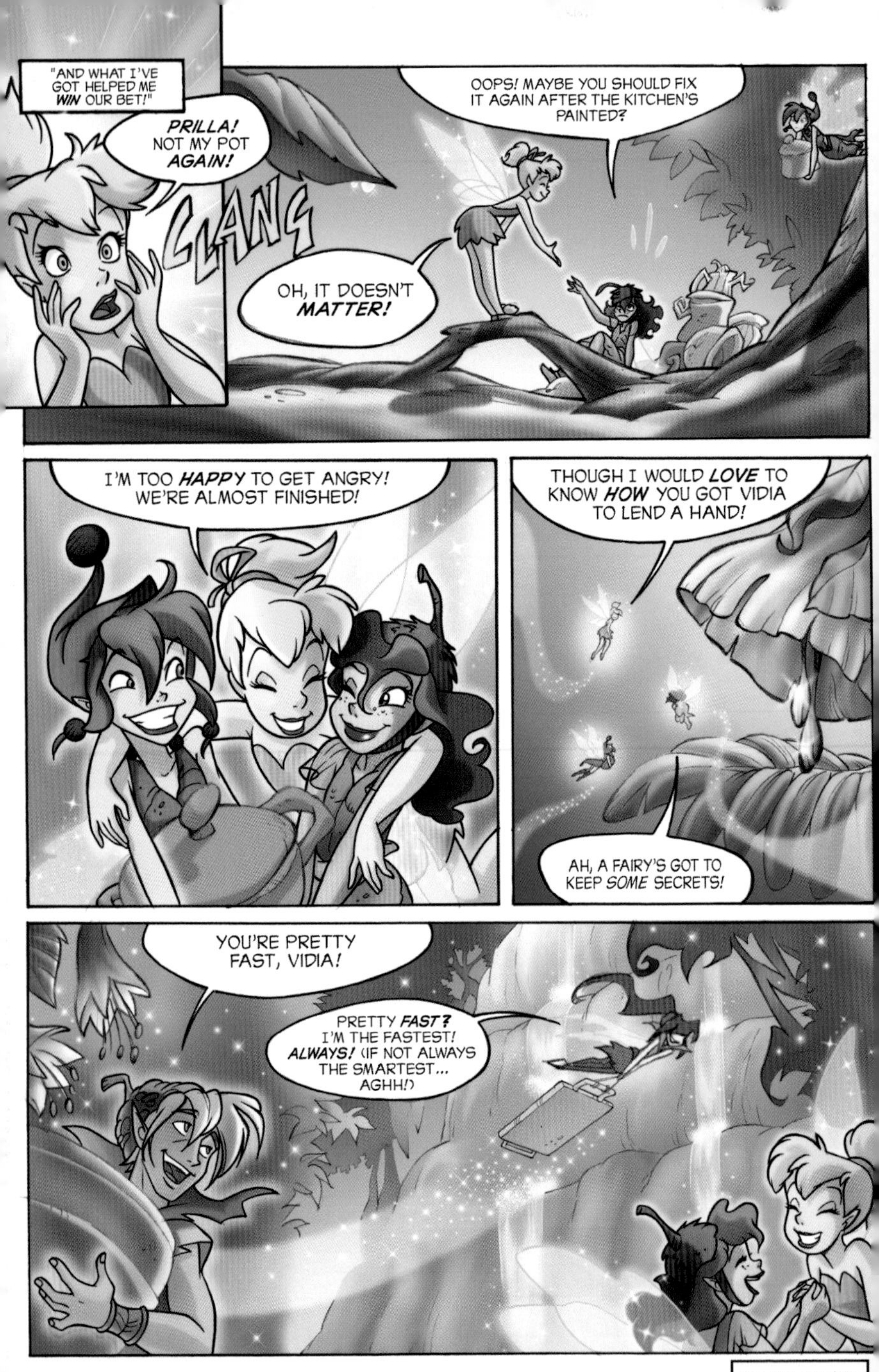
"AND WHAT I'VE GOT HELPED ME WIN OUR BET!"
PRILLA! NOT MY POT AGAIN!
CLANG
OOPS! MAYBE YOU SHOULD FIX IT AGAIN AFTER THE KITCHEN'S PAINTED?
OH, IT DOESN'T MATTER!
I'M TOO HAPPY TO GET ANGRY! WE'RE ALMOST FINISHED!
THOUGH I WOULD LOVE TO KNOW HOW YOU GOT VIDIA TO LEND A HAND!
AH, A FAIRY'S GOT TO KEEP SOME SECRETS!
YOU'RE PRETTY FAST, VIDIA!
PRETTY FAST? I'M THE FASTEST! ALWAYS! (IF NOT ALWAYS THE SMARTEST... AGHH!)

THE END

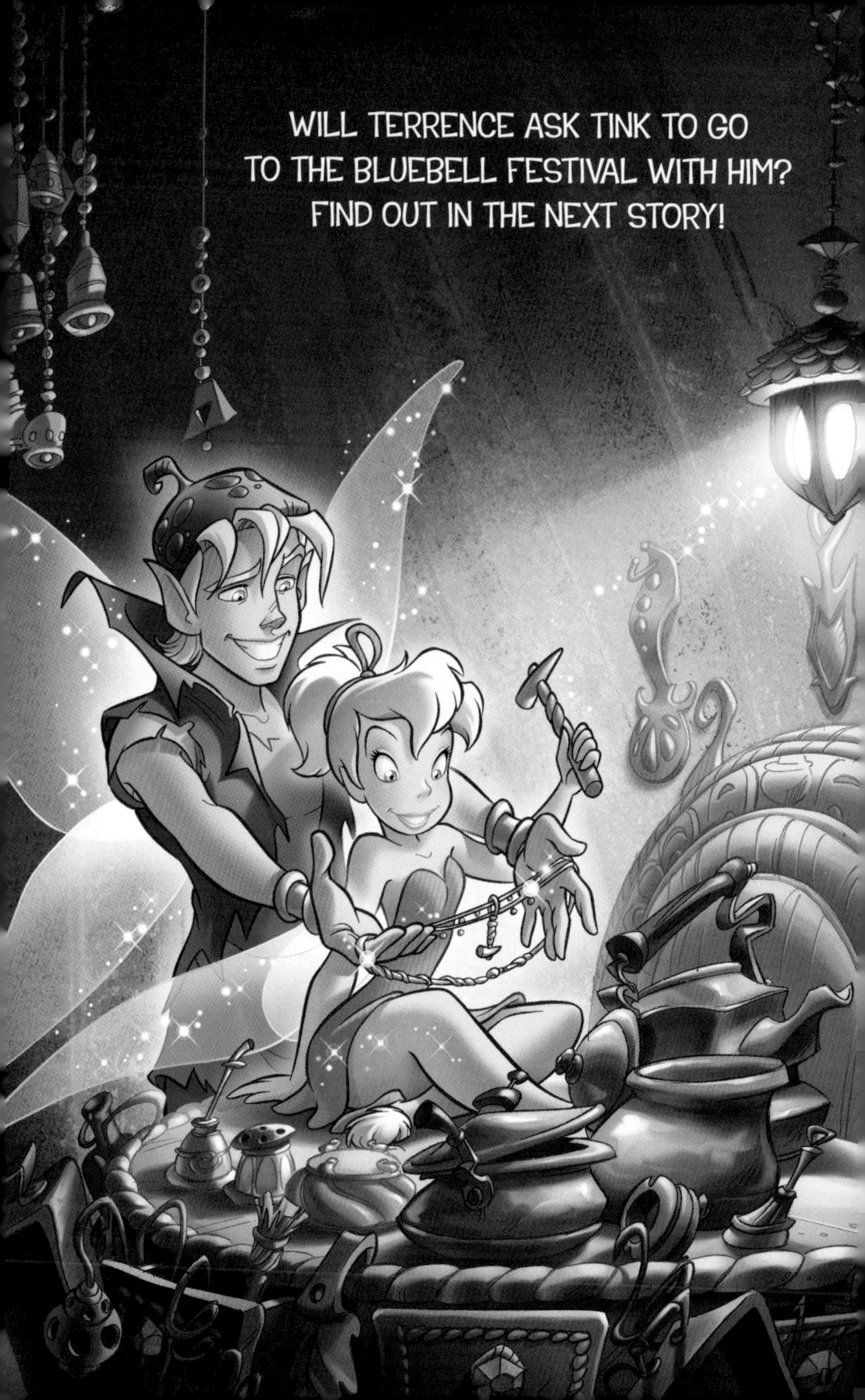
WILL TERRENCE ASK TINK TO GO
TO THE BLUEBELL FESTIVAL WITH HIM?
FIND OUT IN THE NEXT STORY!

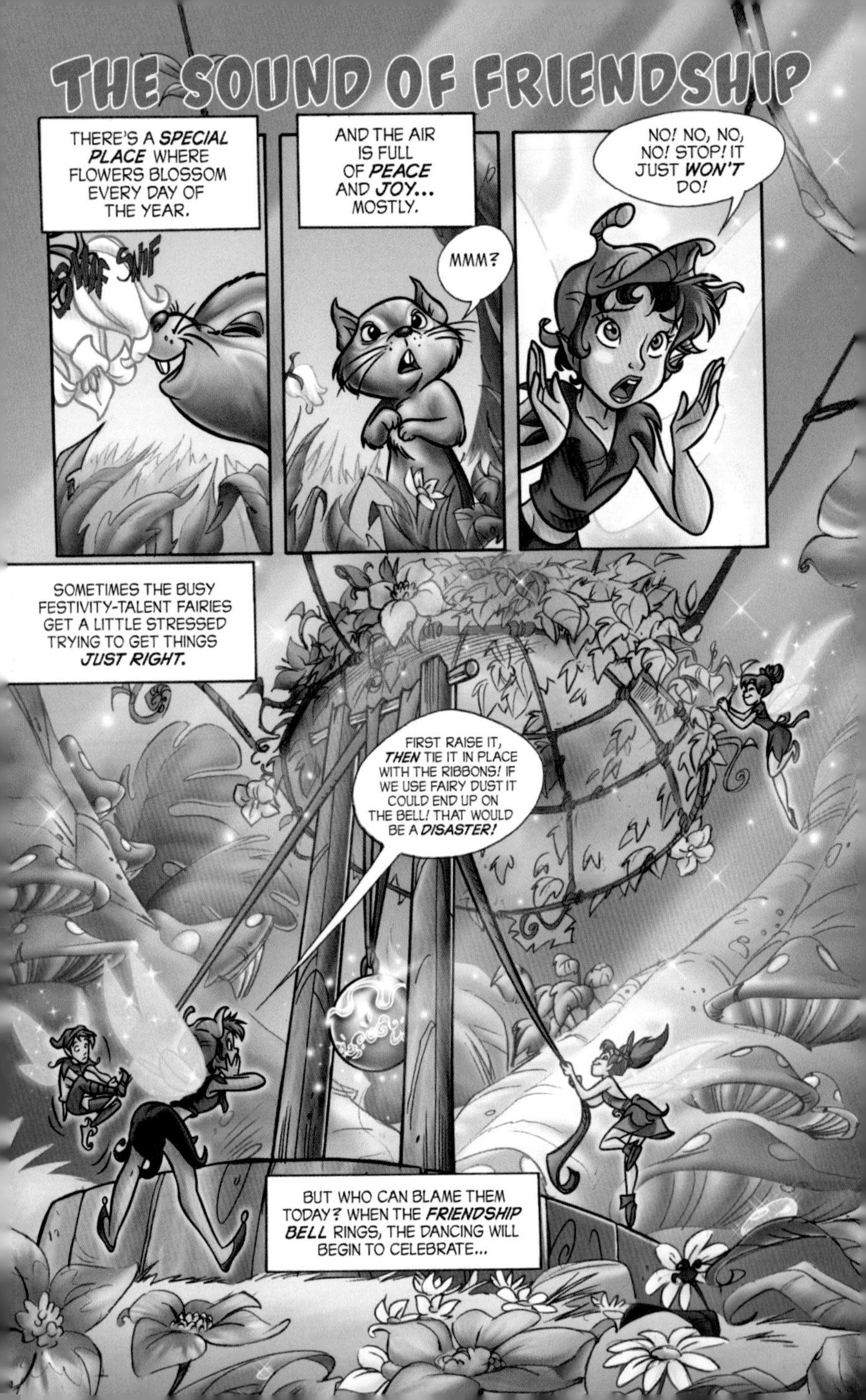
THE SOUND OF FRIENDSHIP
THERE'S A SPECIAL PLACE WHERE FLOWERS BLOSSOM EVERY DAY OF THE YEAR.
SNIF SNIF
AND THE AIR IS FULL OF PEACE AND JOY... MOSTLY.
MMM?
NO! NO, NO, NO! STOP! IT JUST WON'T DO!
SOMETIMES THE BUSY FESTIVITY-TALENT FAIRIES GET A LITTLE STRESSED TRYING TO GET THINGS JUST RIGHT.
FIRST RAISE IT, THEN TIE IT IN PLACE WITH THE RIBBONS! IF WE USE FAIRY DUST IT COULD END UP ON THE BELL! THAT WOULD BE A DISASTER!
BUT WHO CAN BLAME THEM TODAY? WHEN THE FRIENDSHIP BELL RINGS, THE DANCING WILL BEGIN TO CELEBRATE...

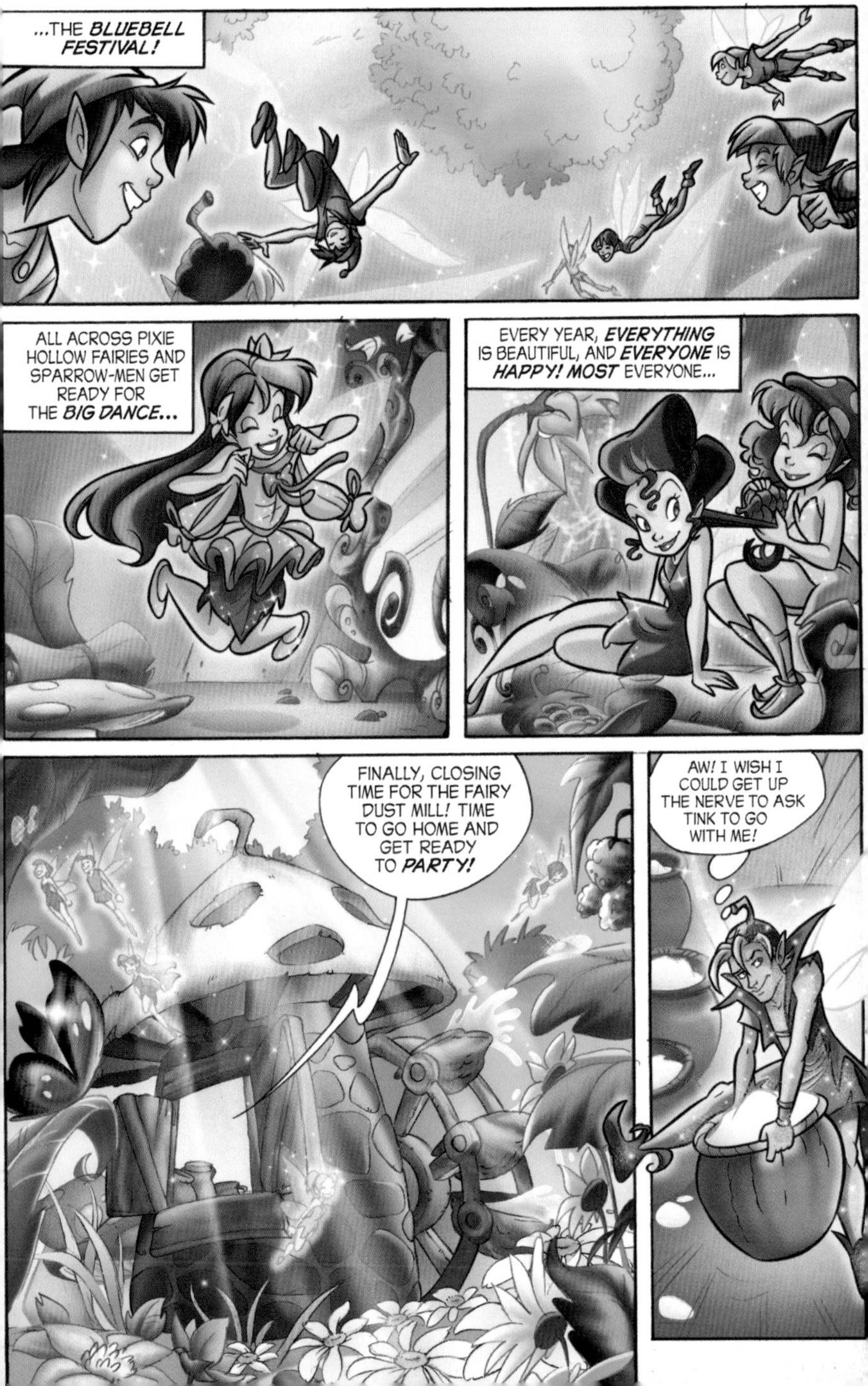
...THE BLUEBELL FESTIVAL!
ALL ACROSS PIXIE HOLLOW FAIRIES AND SPARROW-MEN GET READY FOR THE BIG DANCE...
EVERY YEAR, EVERYTHING IS BEAUTIFUL, AND EVERYONE IS HAPPY! MOST EVERYONE...
FINALLY, CLOSING TIME FOR THE FAIRY DUST MILL! TIME TO GO HOME AND GET READY TO PARTY!
AW! I WISH I COULD GET UP THE NERVE TO ASK TINK TO GO WITH ME!

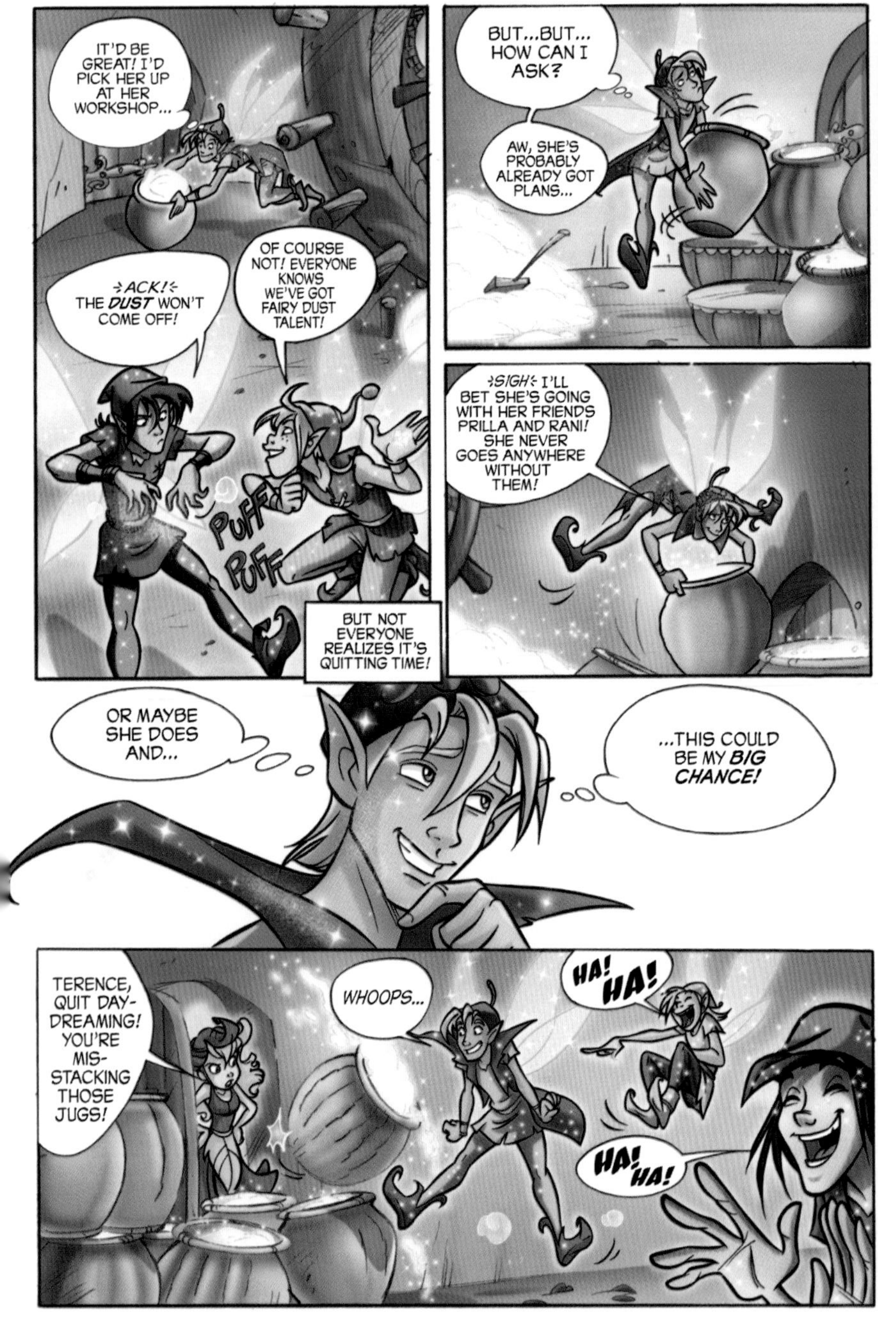

IT'D BE GREAT! I'D PICK HER UP AT HER WORKSHOP...
BUT...BUT... HOW CAN I ASK?
AW, SHE'S PROBABLY ALREADY GOT PLANS...
ACK! THE DUST WON'T COME OFF!
OF COURSE NOT! EVERYONE KNOWS WE'VE GOT FAIRY DUST TALENT!
PUFF PUFF
BUT NOT EVERYONE REALIZES IT'S QUITTING TIME!
SIGH I'LL BET SHE'S GOING WITH HER FRIENDS PRILLA AND RANI! SHE NEVER GOES ANYWHERE WITHOUT THEM!
OR MAYBE SHE DOES AND...
...THIS COULD BE MY BIG CHANCE!
TERENCE, QUIT DAY-DREAMING! YOU'RE MIS-STACKING THOSE JUGS!
WHOOPS...
HA! HA!
HA! HA!

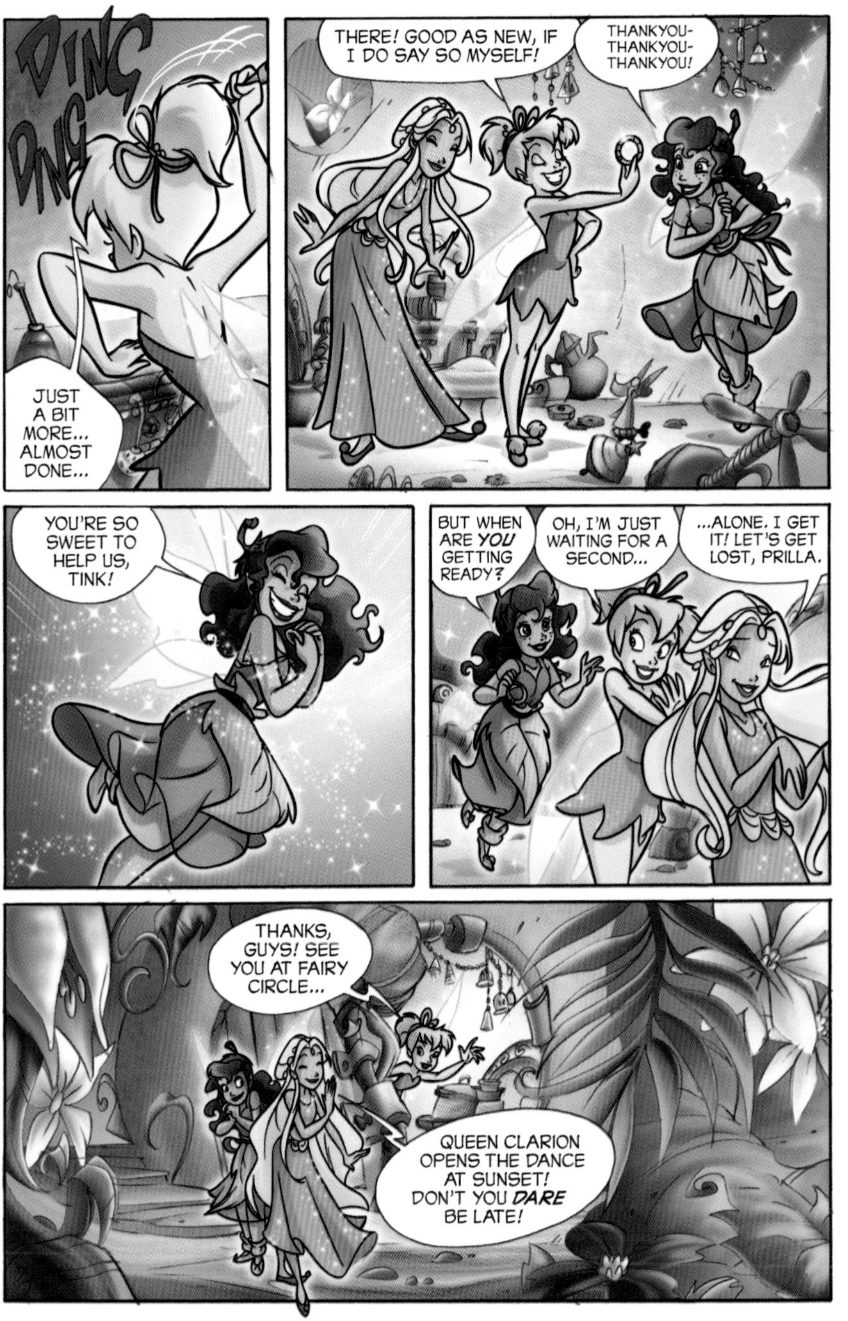
DING
DING
JUST A BIT MORE... ALMOST DONE...
THERE! GOOD AS NEW, IF I DO SAY SO MYSELF!
THANKYOU-THANKYOU-THANKYOU!
YOU'RE SO SWEET TO HELP US, TINK!
BUT WHEN ARE *YOU* GETTING READY?
OH, I'M JUST WAITING FOR A SECOND...
...ALONE. I GET IT! LET'S GET LOST, PRILLA.
THANKS, GUYS! SEE YOU AT FAIRY CIRCLE...
QUEEN CLARION OPENS THE DANCE AT SUNSET! DON'T YOU *DARE* BE LATE!

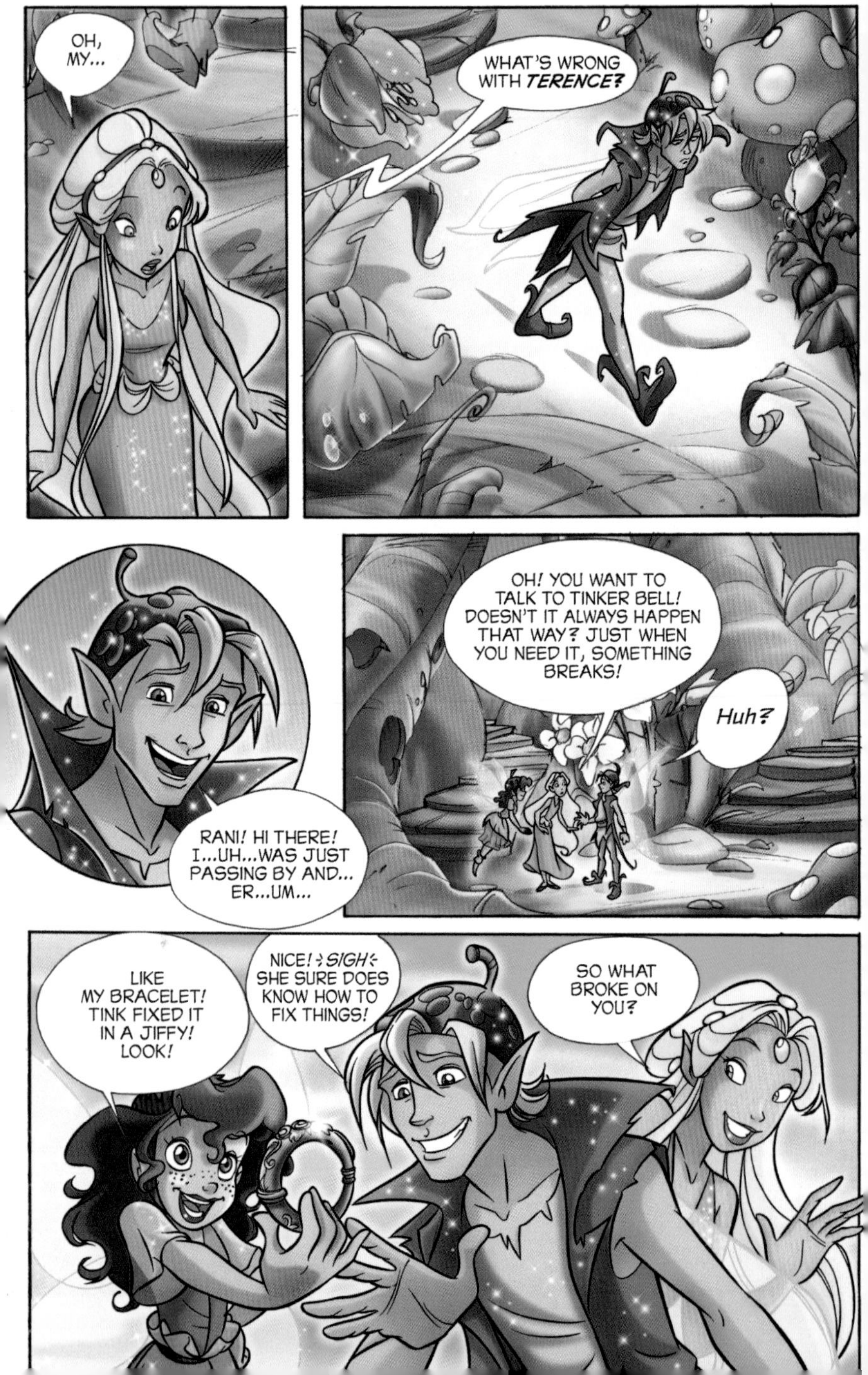

OH, MY...
WHAT'S WRONG WITH *TERENCE?*
RANI! HI THERE! I...UH...WAS JUST PASSING BY AND... ER...UM...
OH! YOU WANT TO TALK TO TINKER BELL! DOESN'T IT ALWAYS HAPPEN THAT WAY? JUST WHEN YOU NEED IT, SOMETHING BREAKS!
Huh?
LIKE MY BRACELET! TINK FIXED IT IN A JIFFY! LOOK!
NICE! *SIGH* SHE SURE DOES KNOW HOW TO FIX THINGS!
SO WHAT BROKE ON YOU?

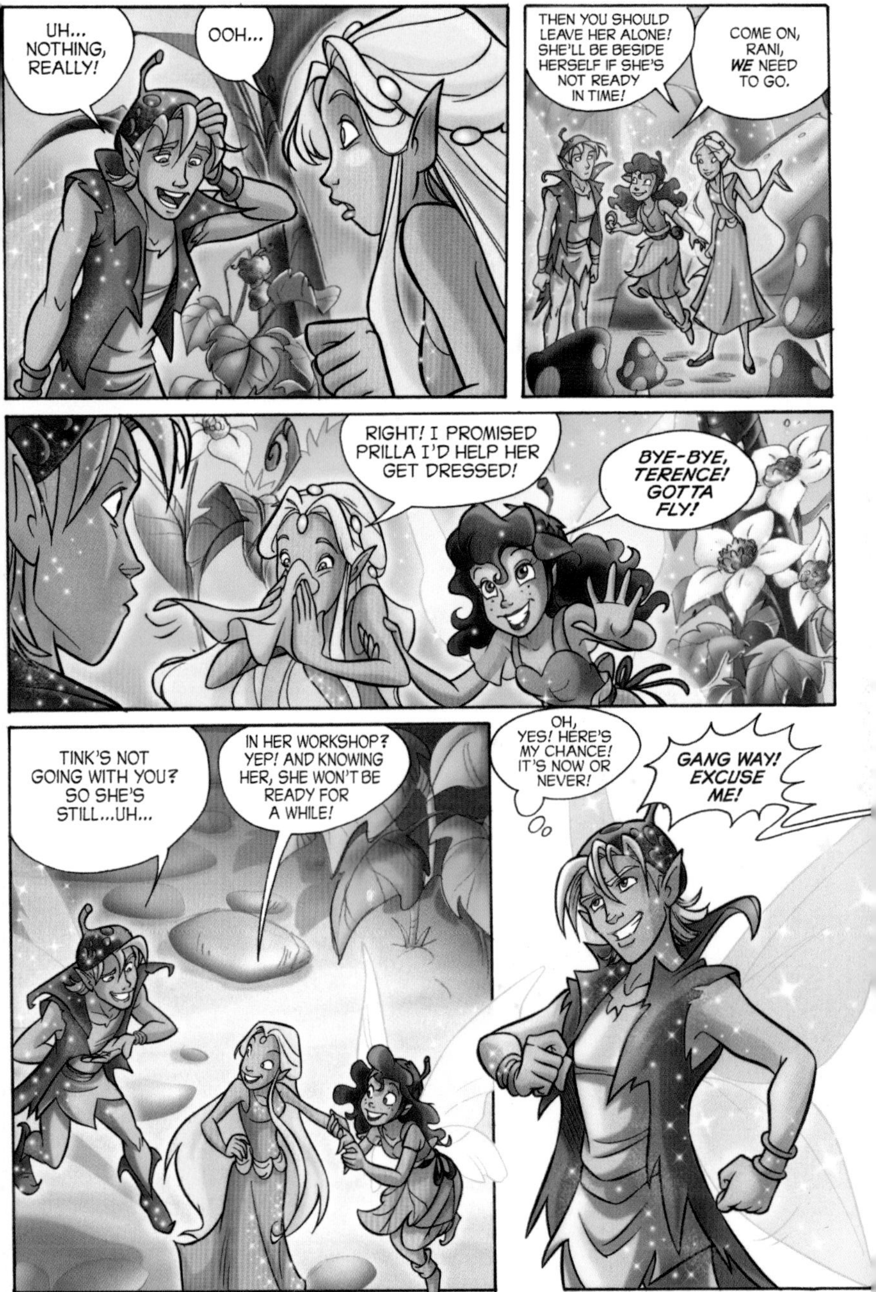
UH... NOTHING, REALLY!
OOH...
THEN YOU SHOULD LEAVE HER ALONE! SHE'LL BE BESIDE HERSELF IF SHE'S NOT READY IN TIME!
COME ON, RANI, *WE* NEED TO GO.
RIGHT! I PROMISED PRILLA I'D HELP HER GET DRESSED!
BYE-BYE, TERENCE! GOTTA FLY!
TINK'S NOT GOING WITH YOU? SO SHE'S STILL...UH...
IN HER WORKSHOP? YEP! AND KNOWING HER, SHE WON'T BE READY FOR A WHILE!
OH, YES! HERE'S MY CHANCE! IT'S NOW OR NEVER!
GANG WAY! EXCUSE ME!

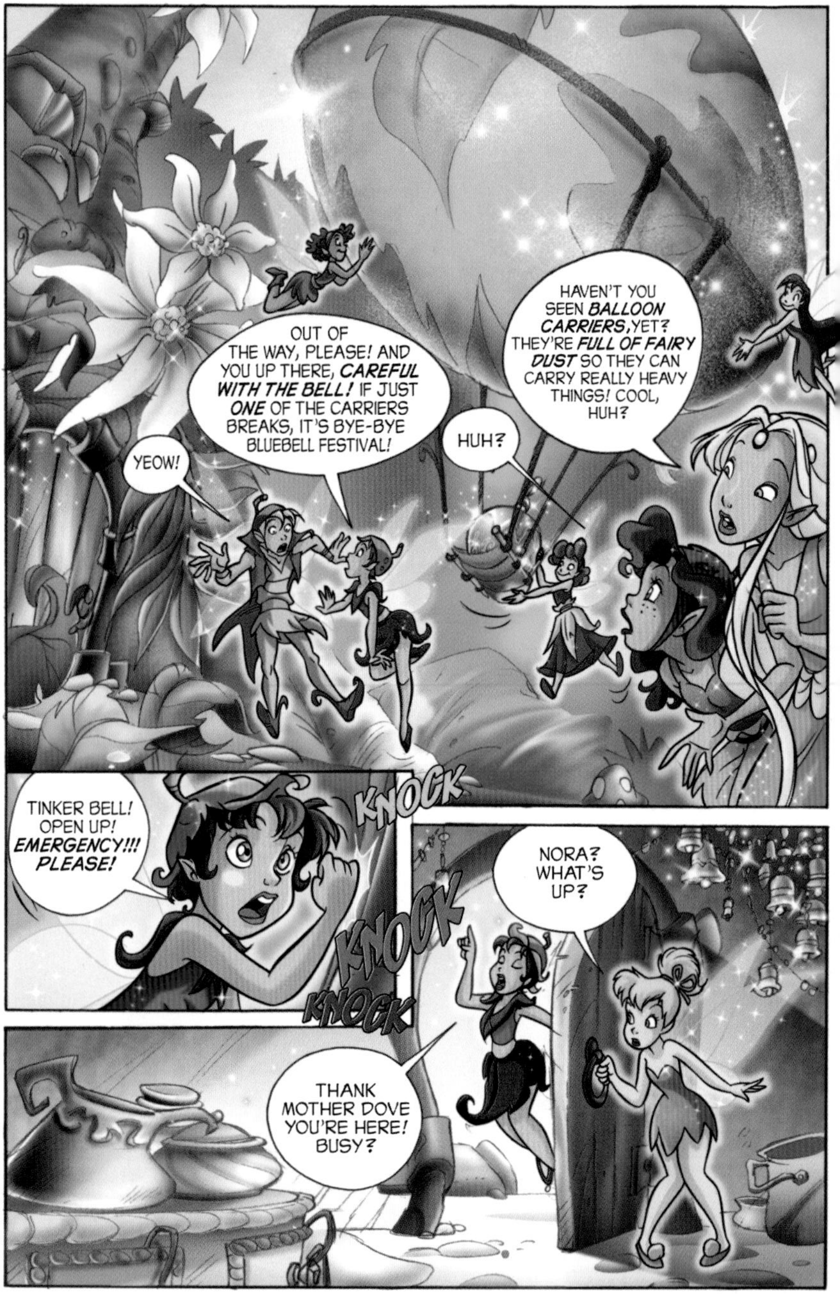
OUT OF THE WAY, PLEASE! AND YOU UP THERE, CAREFUL WITH THE BELL! IF JUST ONE OF THE CARRIERS BREAKS, IT'S BYE-BYE BLUEBELL FESTIVAL!
YEOW!
HUH?
HAVEN'T YOU SEEN BALLOON CARRIERS, YET? THEY'RE FULL OF FAIRY DUST SO THEY CAN CARRY REALLY HEAVY THINGS! COOL, HUH?
TINKER BELL! OPEN UP! EMERGENCY!!! PLEASE!
KNOCK
KNOCK
KNOCK
NORA? WHAT'S UP?
THANK MOTHER DOVE YOU'RE HERE! BUSY?

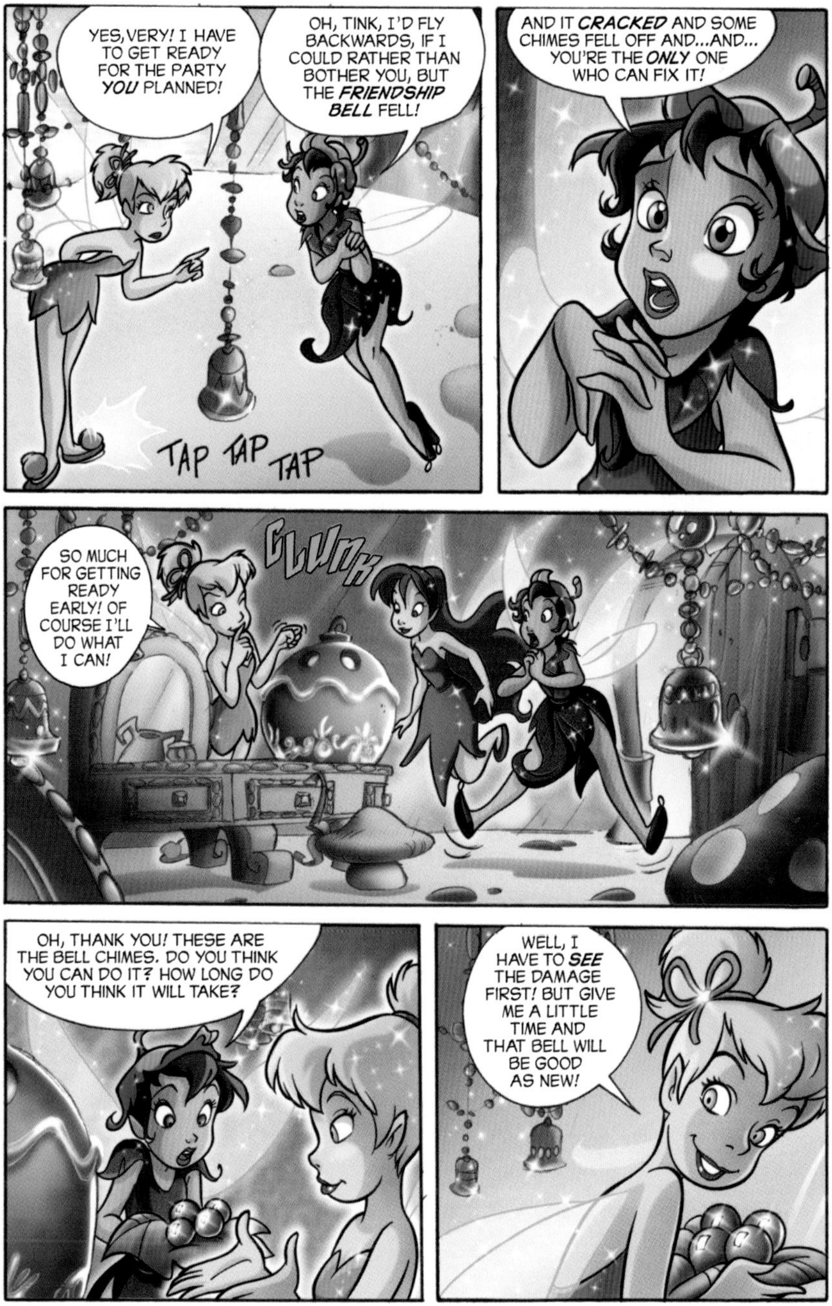
YES, VERY! I HAVE TO GET READY FOR THE PARTY YOU PLANNED!
OH, TINK, I'D FLY BACKWARDS, IF I COULD RATHER THAN BOTHER YOU, BUT THE FRIENDSHIP BELL FELL!
TAP TAP TAP
AND IT CRACKED AND SOME CHIMES FELL OFF AND...AND... YOU'RE THE ONLY ONE WHO CAN FIX IT!
SO MUCH FOR GETTING READY EARLY! OF COURSE I'LL DO WHAT I CAN!
CLUNK
OH, THANK YOU! THESE ARE THE BELL CHIMES. DO YOU THINK YOU CAN DO IT? HOW LONG DO YOU THINK IT WILL TAKE?
WELL, I HAVE TO SEE THE DAMAGE FIRST! BUT GIVE ME A LITTLE TIME AND THAT BELL WILL BE GOOD AS NEW!

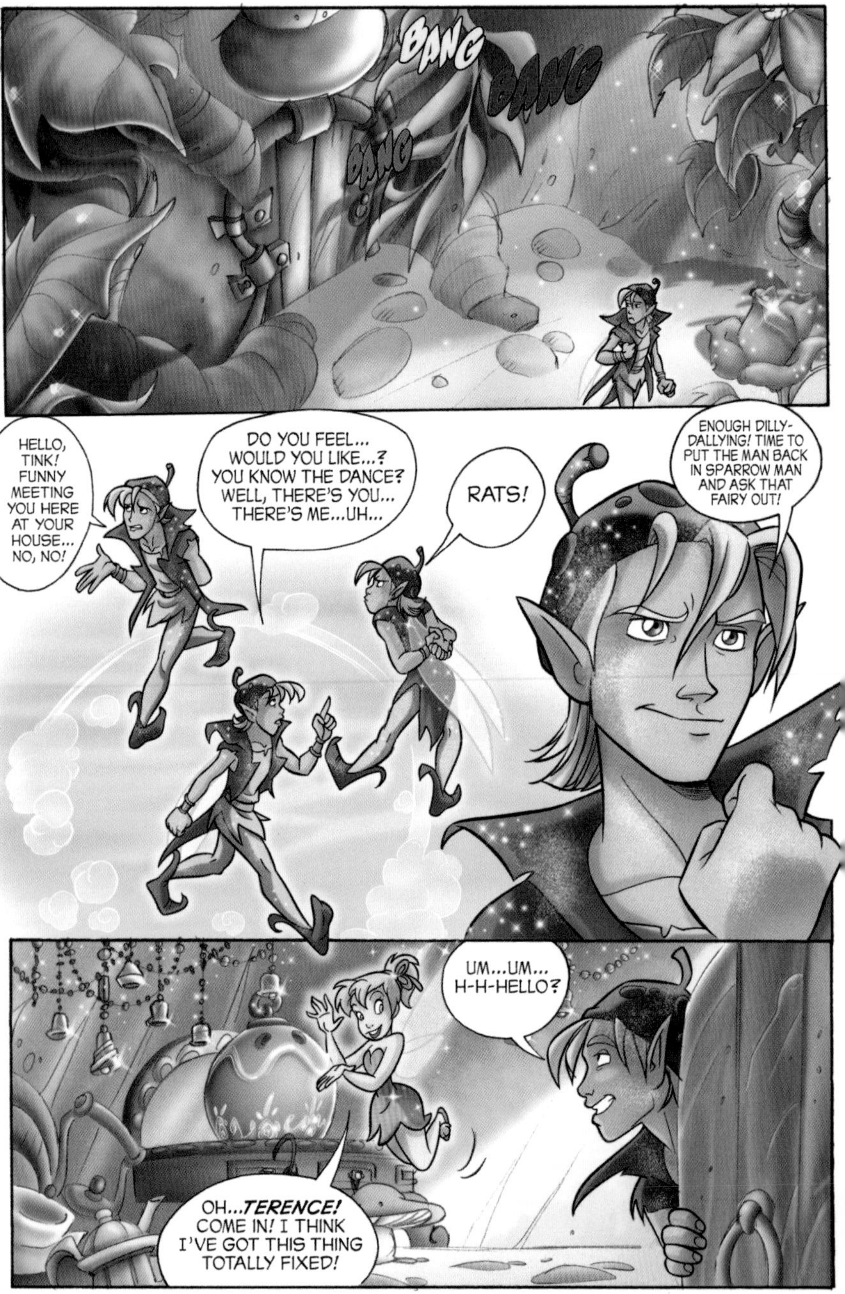
BANG
BANG
BANG
HELLO, TINK! FUNNY MEETING YOU HERE AT YOUR HOUSE... NO, NO!
DO YOU FEEL... WOULD YOU LIKE...? YOU KNOW THE DANCE? WELL, THERE'S YOU... THERE'S ME...UH...
RATS!
ENOUGH DILLY-DALLYING! TIME TO PUT THE MAN BACK IN SPARROW MAN AND ASK THAT FAIRY OUT!
UM...UM... H-H-HELLO?
OH...*TERENCE!* COME IN! I THINK I'VE GOT THIS THING TOTALLY FIXED!

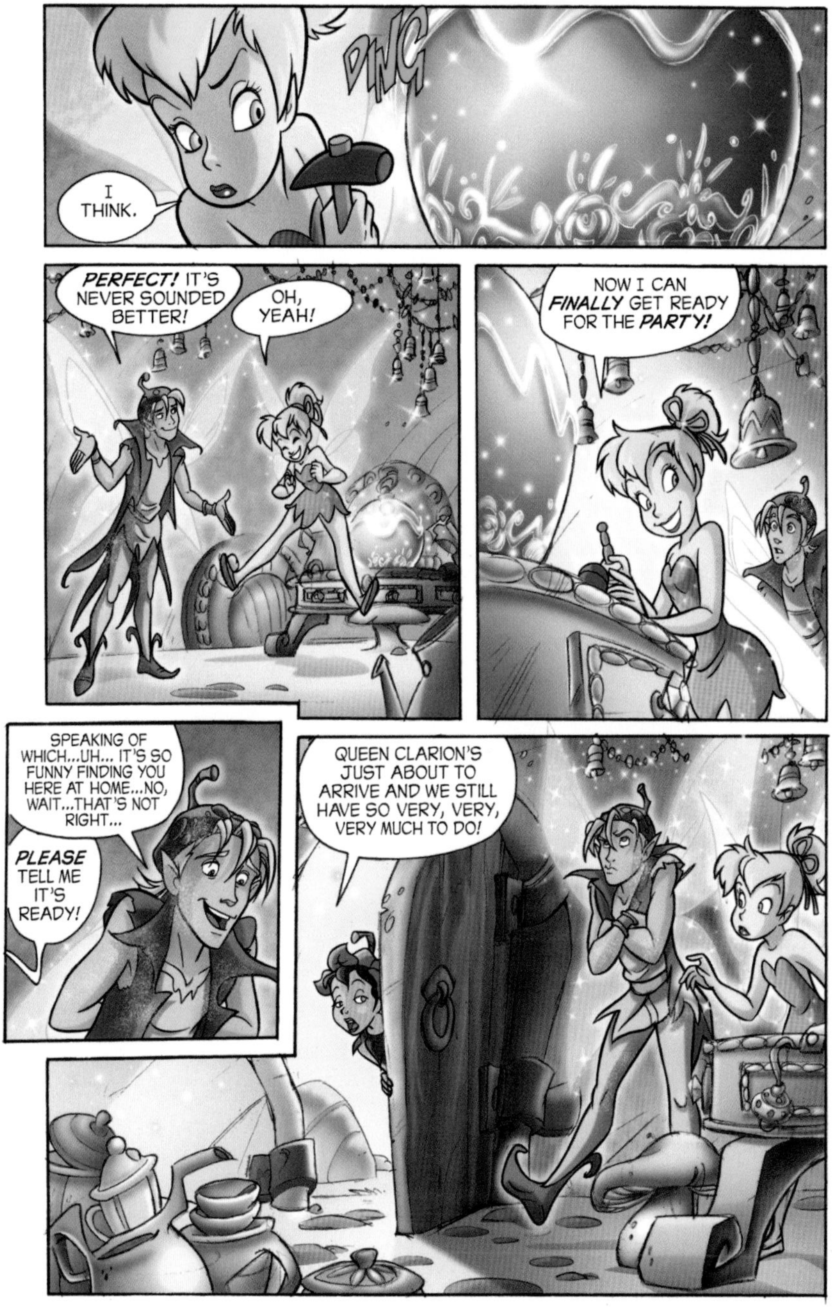
DING
I THINK.
PERFECT! IT'S NEVER SOUNDED BETTER!
OH, YEAH!
NOW I CAN FINALLY GET READY FOR THE PARTY!
SPEAKING OF WHICH...UH... IT'S SO FUNNY FINDING YOU HERE AT HOME...NO, WAIT...THAT'S NOT RIGHT...
PLEASE TELL ME IT'S READY!
QUEEN CLARION'S JUST ABOUT TO ARRIVE AND WE STILL HAVE SO VERY, VERY, VERY MUCH TO DO!

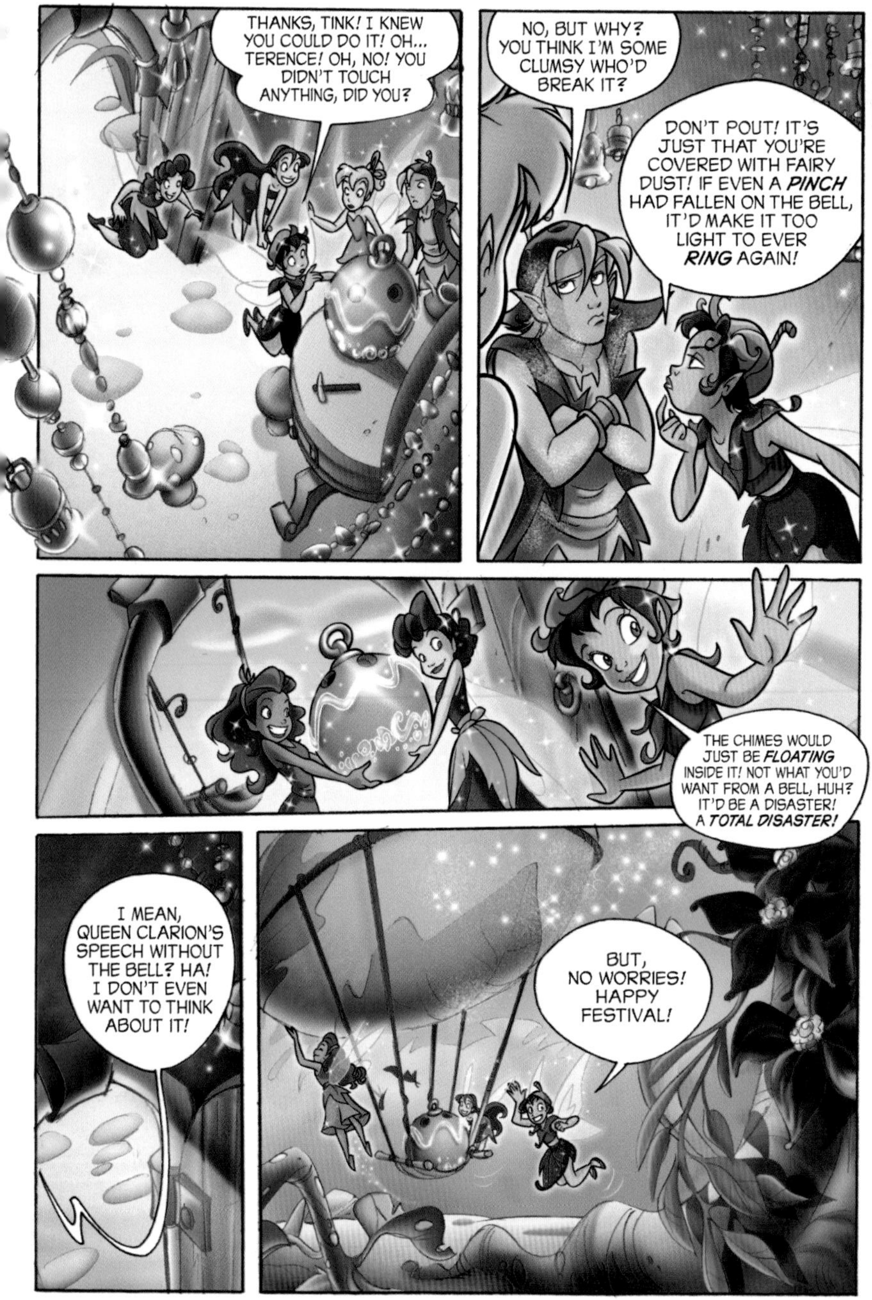
THANKS, TINK! I KNEW YOU COULD DO IT! OH... TERENCE! OH, NO! YOU DIDN'T TOUCH ANYTHING, DID YOU?
NO, BUT WHY? YOU THINK I'M SOME CLUMSY WHO'D BREAK IT?
DON'T POUT! IT'S JUST THAT YOU'RE COVERED WITH FAIRY DUST! IF EVEN A PINCH HAD FALLEN ON THE BELL, IT'D MAKE IT TOO LIGHT TO EVER RING AGAIN!
THE CHIMES WOULD JUST BE FLOATING INSIDE IT! NOT WHAT YOU'D WANT FROM A BELL, HUH? IT'D BE A DISASTER! A TOTAL DISASTER!
I MEAN, QUEEN CLARION'S SPEECH WITHOUT THE BELL? HA! I DON'T EVEN WANT TO THINK ABOUT IT!
BUT, NO WORRIES! HAPPY FESTIVAL!

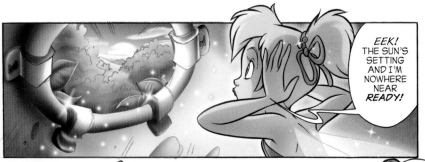

EEK! THE SUN'S SETTING AND I'M NOWHERE NEAR *READY!*

BUT ...!?

FUNNY... THE BELL'S CHIMES ARE STILL HERE!

BETTER TAKE THEM TO NORA, SO TINK CAN FINISH GETTING READY!

WAIT! I *CAN'T* TOUCH THEM! I'M COVERED IN FAIRY DUST!

DRAT!

SORRY, TINK, BUT THERE'S *ANOTHER EMERGENCY!*

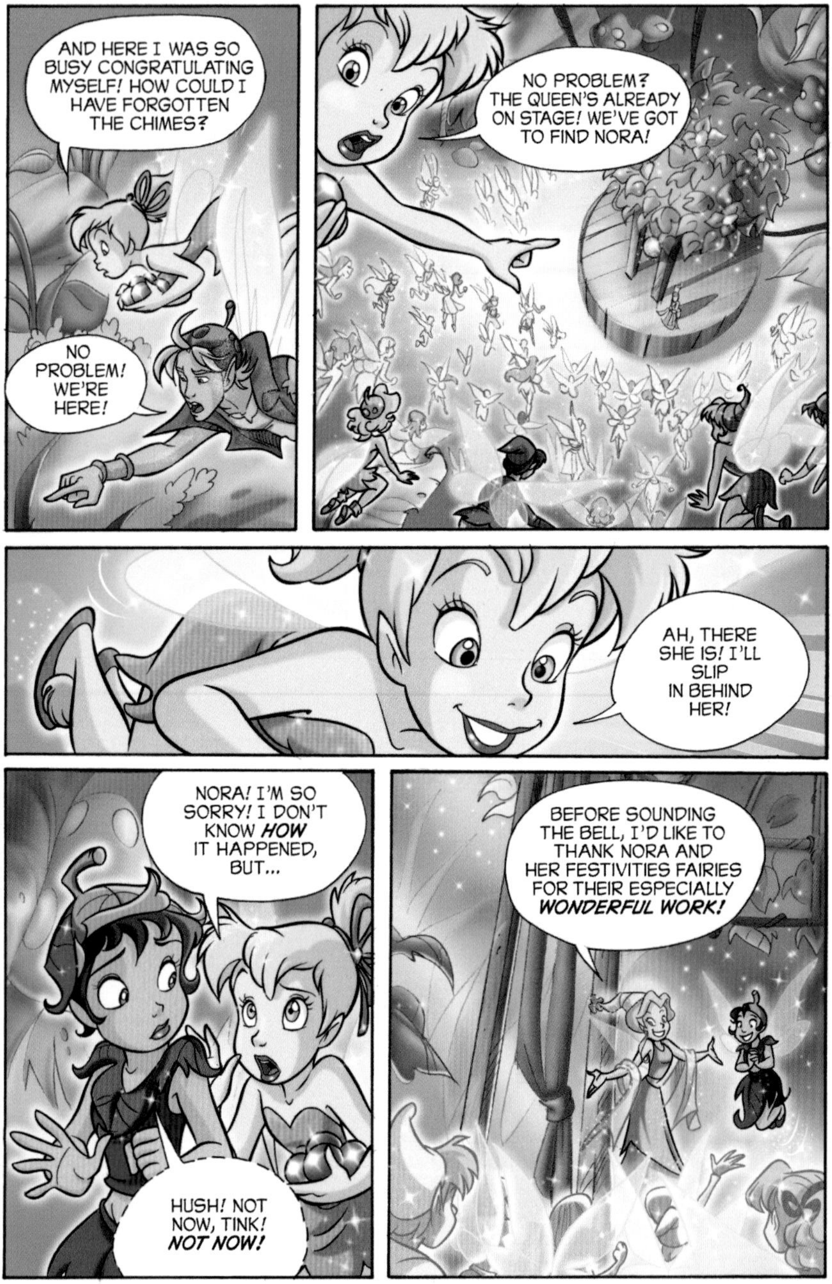
AND HERE I WAS SO BUSY CONGRATULATING MYSELF! HOW COULD I HAVE FORGOTTEN THE CHIMES?
NO PROBLEM! WE'RE HERE!
NO PROBLEM? THE QUEEN'S ALREADY ON STAGE! WE'VE GOT TO FIND NORA!
AH, THERE SHE IS! I'LL SLIP IN BEHIND HER!
NORA! I'M SO SORRY! I DON'T KNOW **HOW** IT HAPPENED, BUT...
HUSH! NOT NOW, TINK! ***NOT NOW!***
BEFORE SOUNDING THE BELL, I'D LIKE TO THANK NORA AND HER FESTIVITIES FAIRIES FOR THEIR ESPECIALLY ***WONDERFUL WORK!***

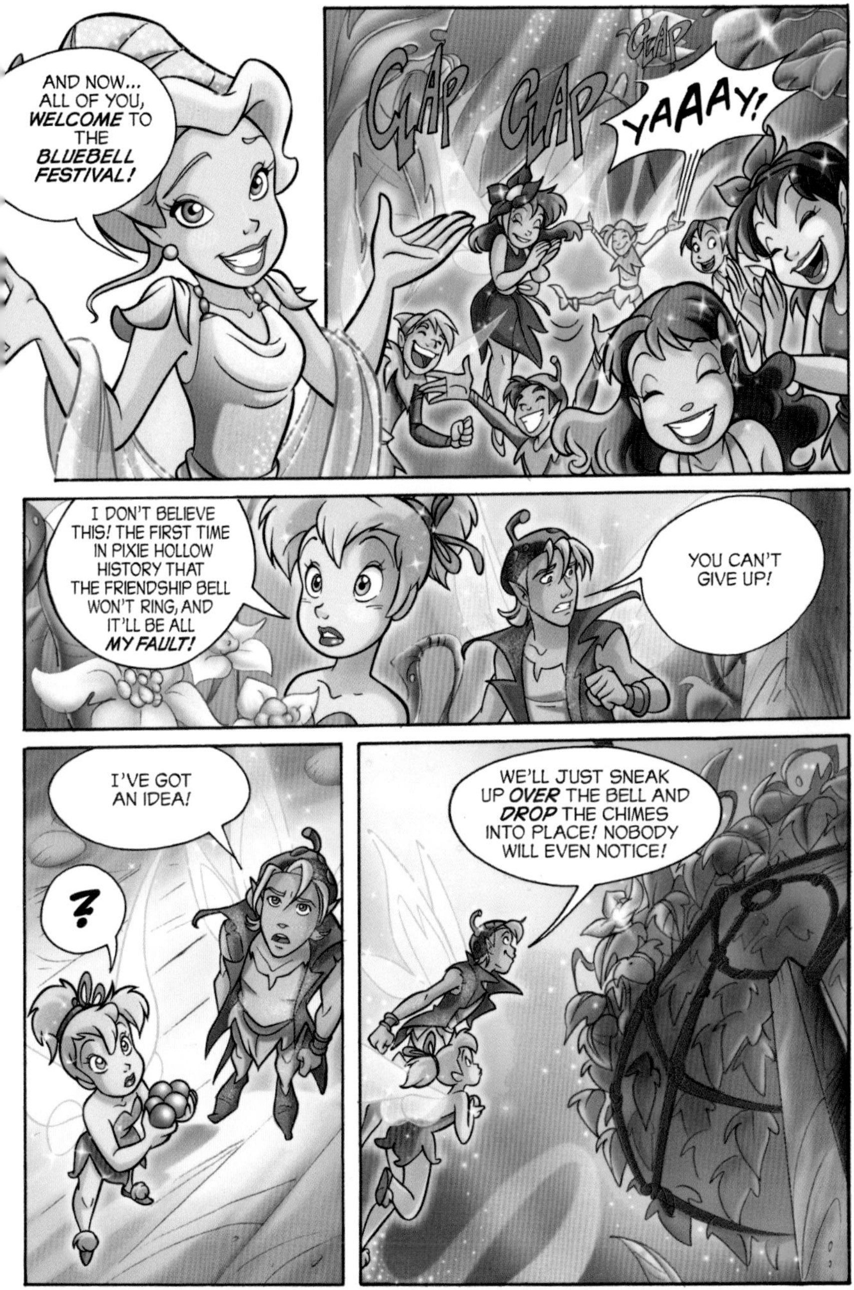
AND NOW... ALL OF YOU, ***WELCOME*** TO THE ***BLUEBELL FESTIVAL!***
CLAP CLAP CLAP
YAAAY!
I DON'T BELIEVE THIS! THE FIRST TIME IN PIXIE HOLLOW HISTORY THAT THE FRIENDSHIP BELL WON'T RING, AND IT'LL BE ALL ***MY FAULT!***
YOU CAN'T GIVE UP!
I'VE GOT AN IDEA!
?
WE'LL JUST SNEAK UP ***OVER*** THE BELL AND ***DROP*** THE CHIMES INTO PLACE! NOBODY WILL EVEN NOTICE!

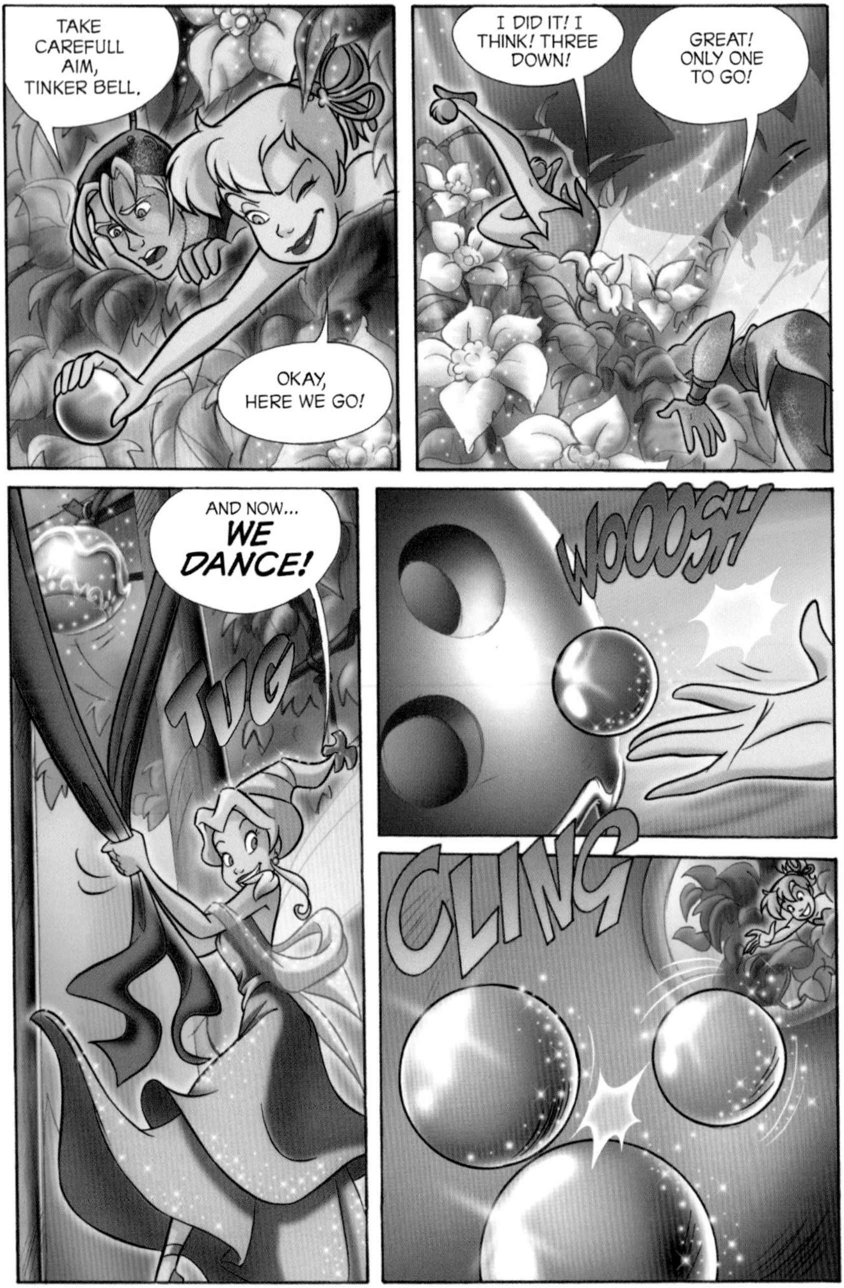
TAKE CAREFULL AIM, TINKER BELL.
OKAY, HERE WE GO!
I DID IT! I THINK! THREE DOWN!
GREAT! ONLY ONE TO GO!
AND NOW... WE DANCE!
TUG
WOOOSH
CLING

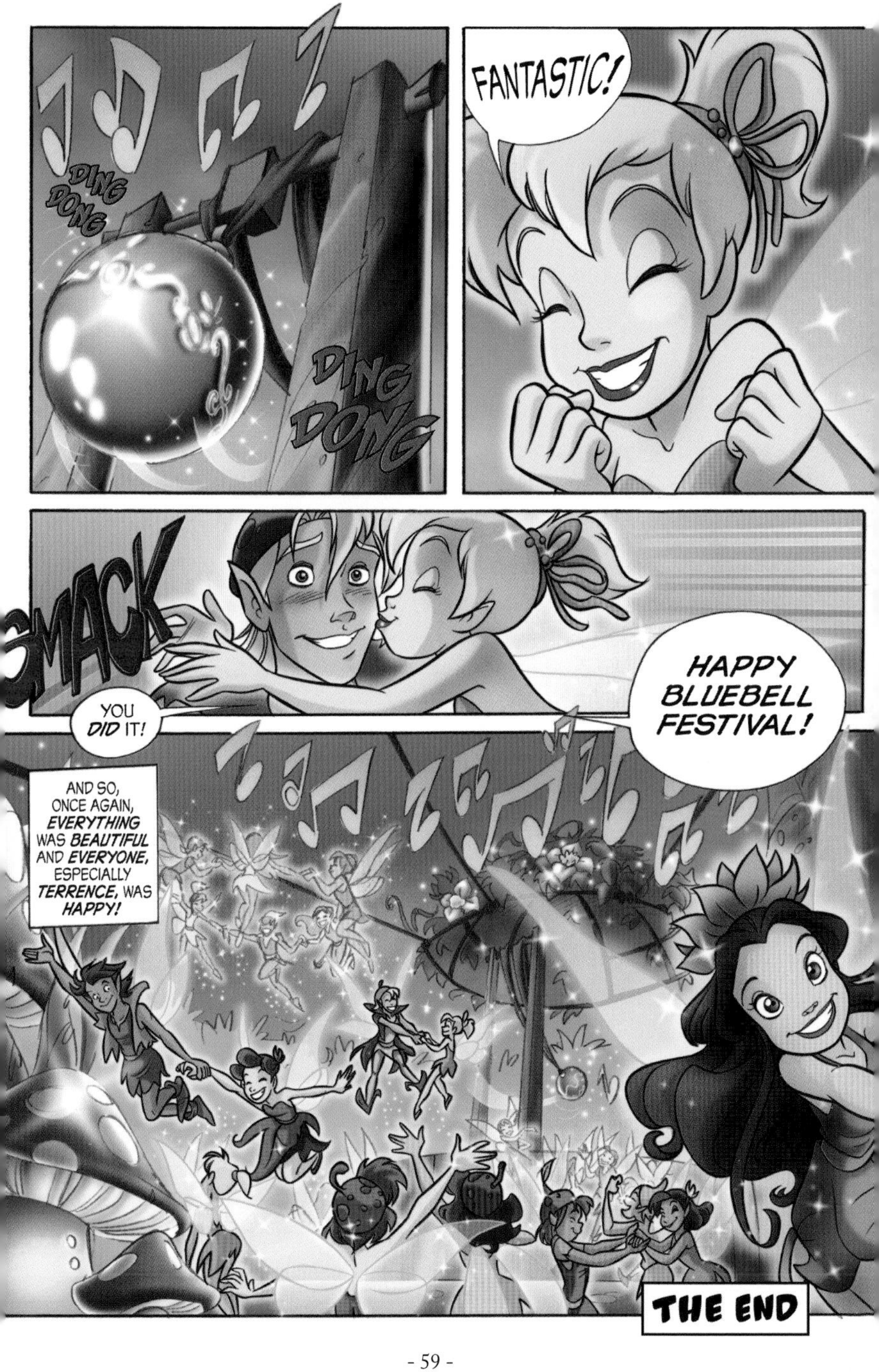

DING DONG
DING DONG
FANTASTIC!
SMACK
YOU DID IT!
HAPPY BLUEBELL FESTIVAL!
AND SO, ONCE AGAIN, EVERYTHING WAS BEAUTIFUL AND EVERYONE, ESPECIALLY TERRENCE, WAS HAPPY!
THE END

THINK TINKER BELL AND RANI
ARE BEST FRIENDS FOREVER?
DON'T BE SO SURE - SEE WHAT HAPPENS
IN THE FOLLOWING STORY!

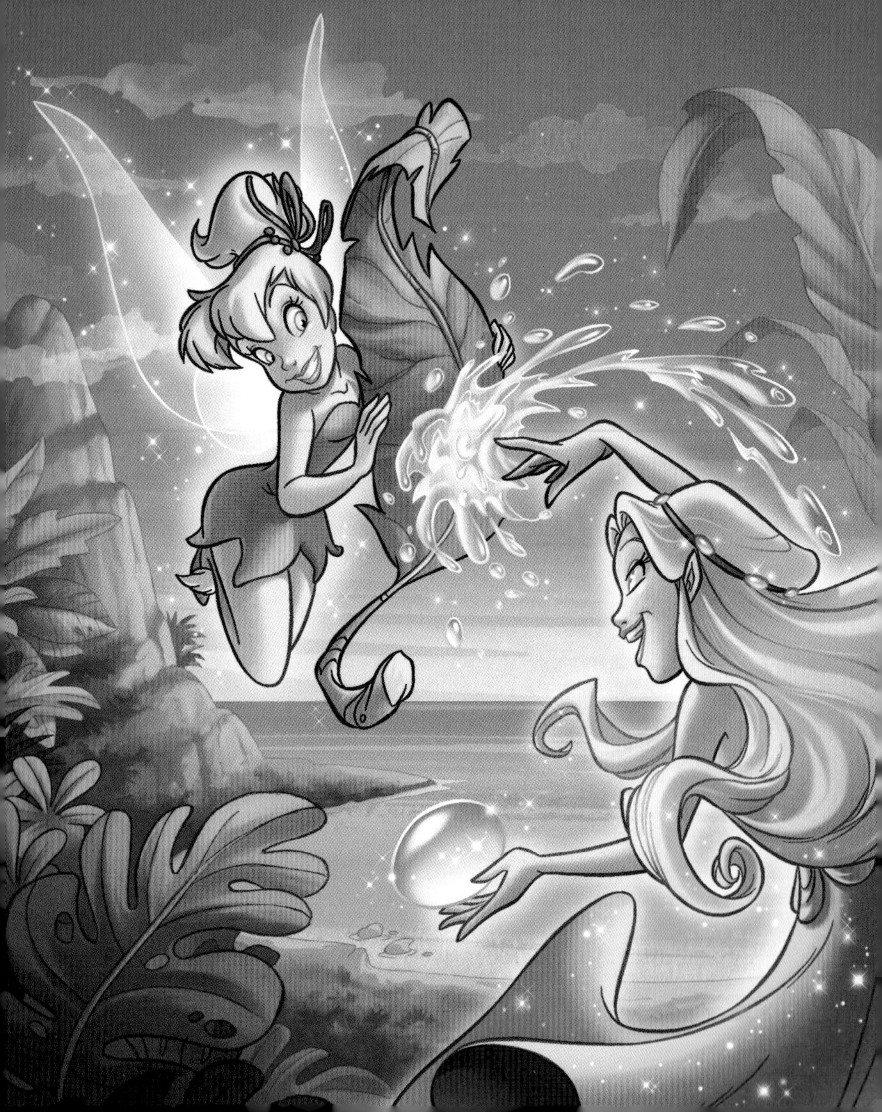

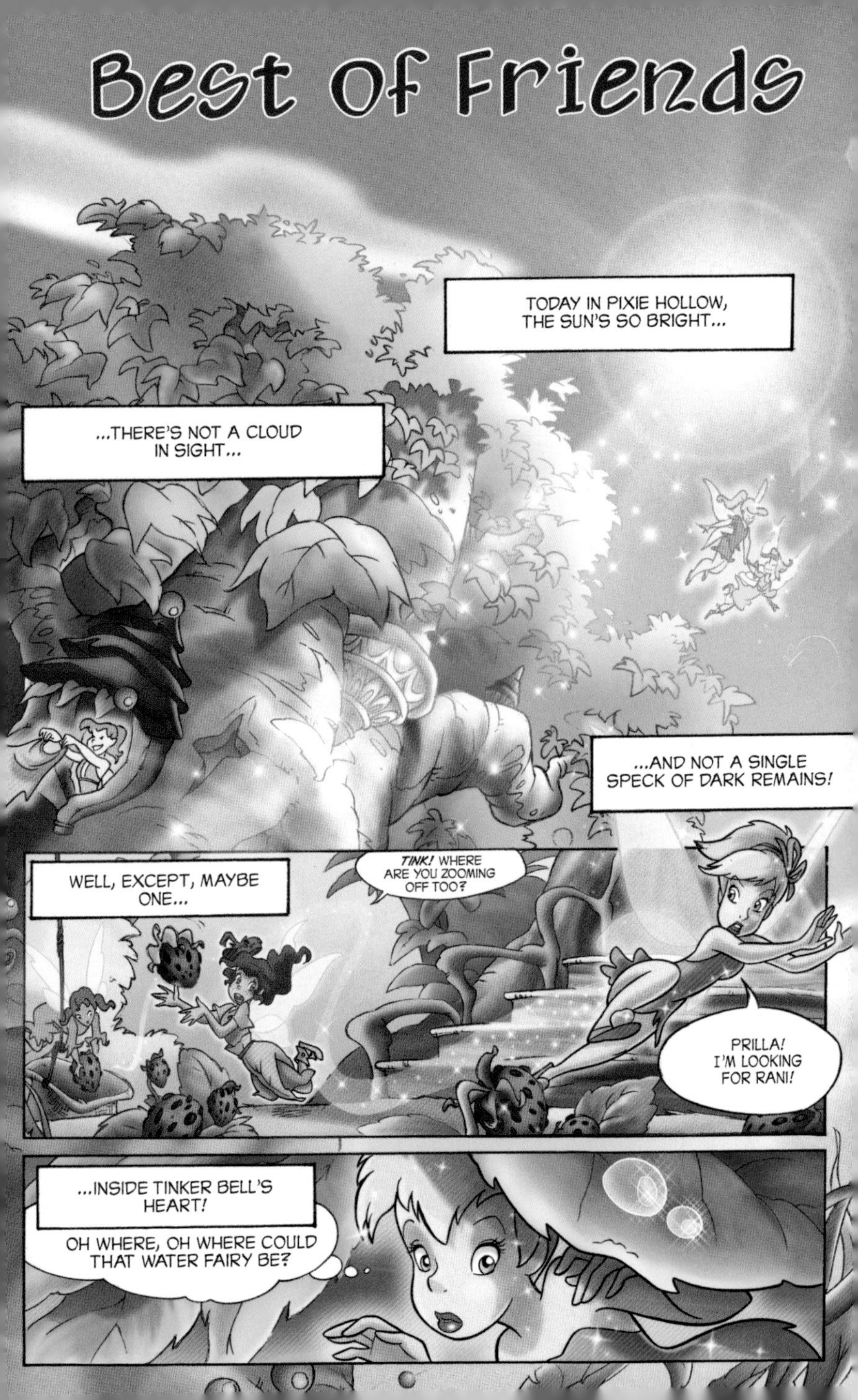
Best Of Friends
TODAY IN PIXIE HOLLOW, THE SUN'S SO BRIGHT...
...THERE'S NOT A CLOUD IN SIGHT...
...AND NOT A SINGLE SPECK OF DARK REMAINS!
WELL, EXCEPT, MAYBE ONE...
TINK! WHERE ARE YOU ZOOMING OFF TOO?
PRILLA! I'M LOOKING FOR RANI!
...INSIDE TINKER BELL'S HEART!
OH WHERE, OH WHERE COULD THAT WATER FAIRY BE?

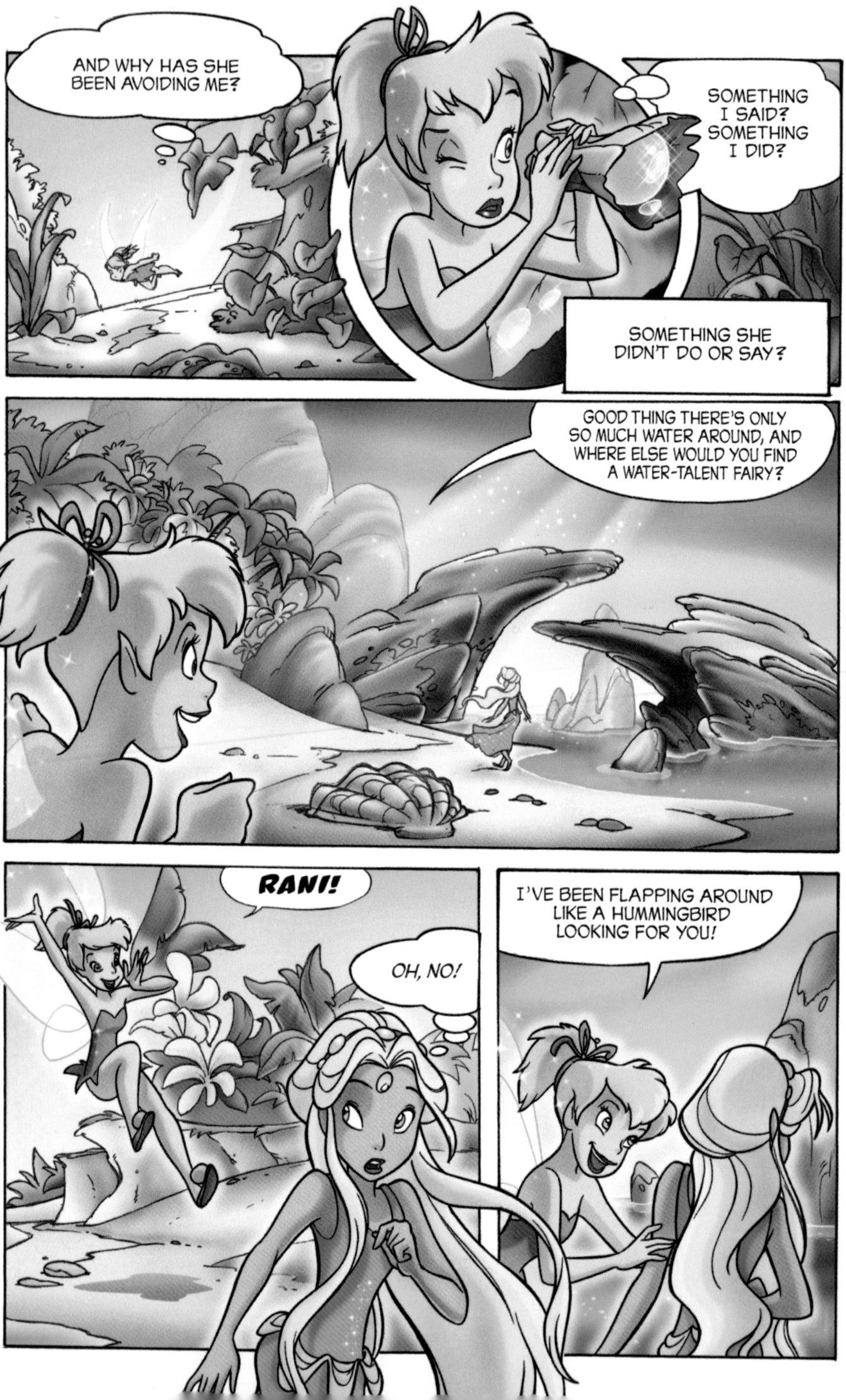
AND WHY HAS SHE BEEN AVOIDING ME?
SOMETHING I SAID? SOMETHING I DID?
SOMETHING SHE DIDN'T DO OR SAY?
GOOD THING THERE'S ONLY SO MUCH WATER AROUND, AND WHERE ELSE WOULD YOU FIND A WATER-TALENT FAIRY?
RANI!
OH, NO!
I'VE BEEN FLAPPING AROUND LIKE A HUMMINGBIRD LOOKING FOR YOU!

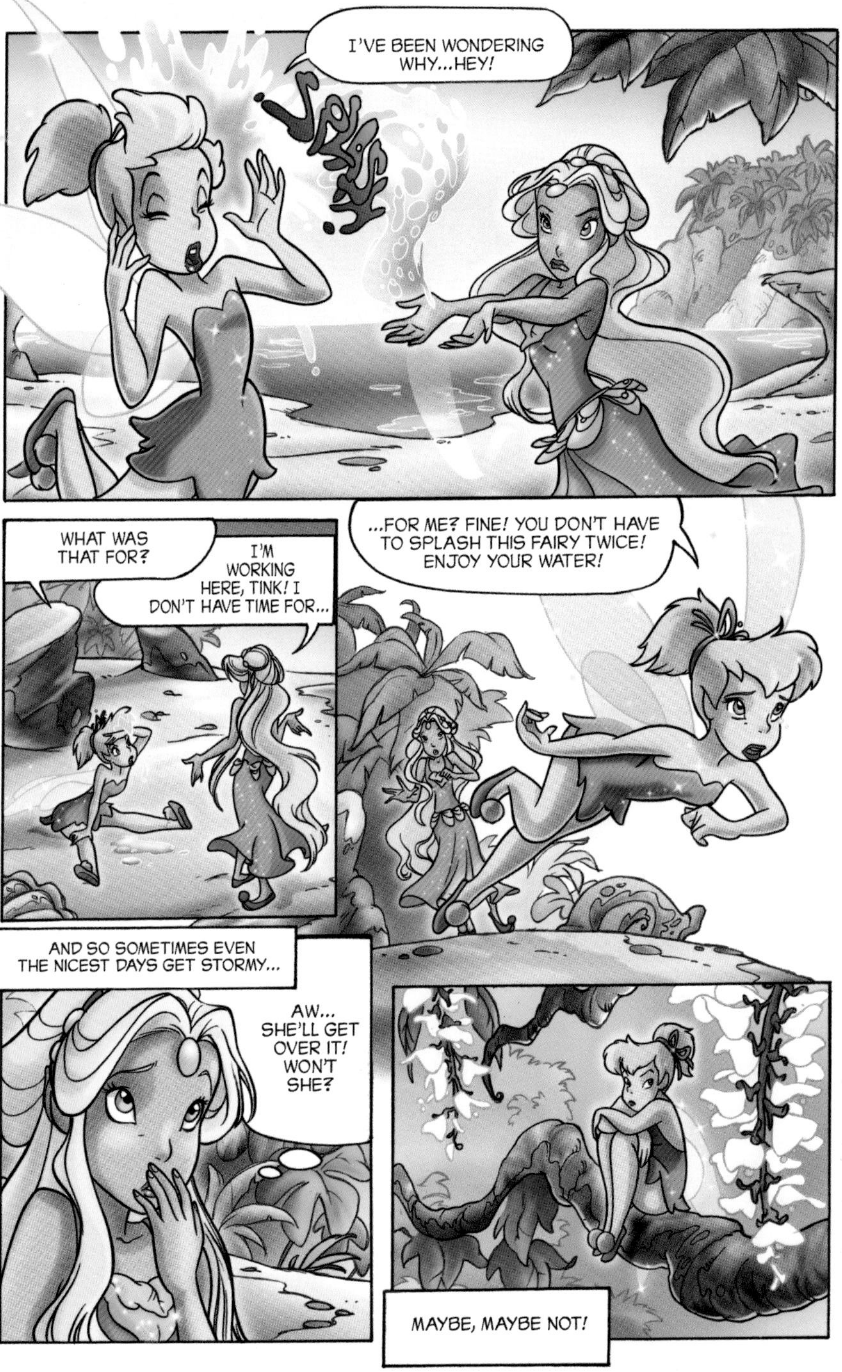
I'VE BEEN WONDERING WHY...HEY!
SPLASH!
WHAT WAS THAT FOR?
I'M WORKING HERE, TINK! I DON'T HAVE TIME FOR...
...FOR ME? FINE! YOU DON'T HAVE TO SPLASH THIS FAIRY TWICE! ENJOY YOUR WATER!
AND SO SOMETIMES EVEN THE NICEST DAYS GET STORMY...
AW... SHE'LL GET OVER IT! WON'T SHE?
MAYBE, MAYBE NOT!

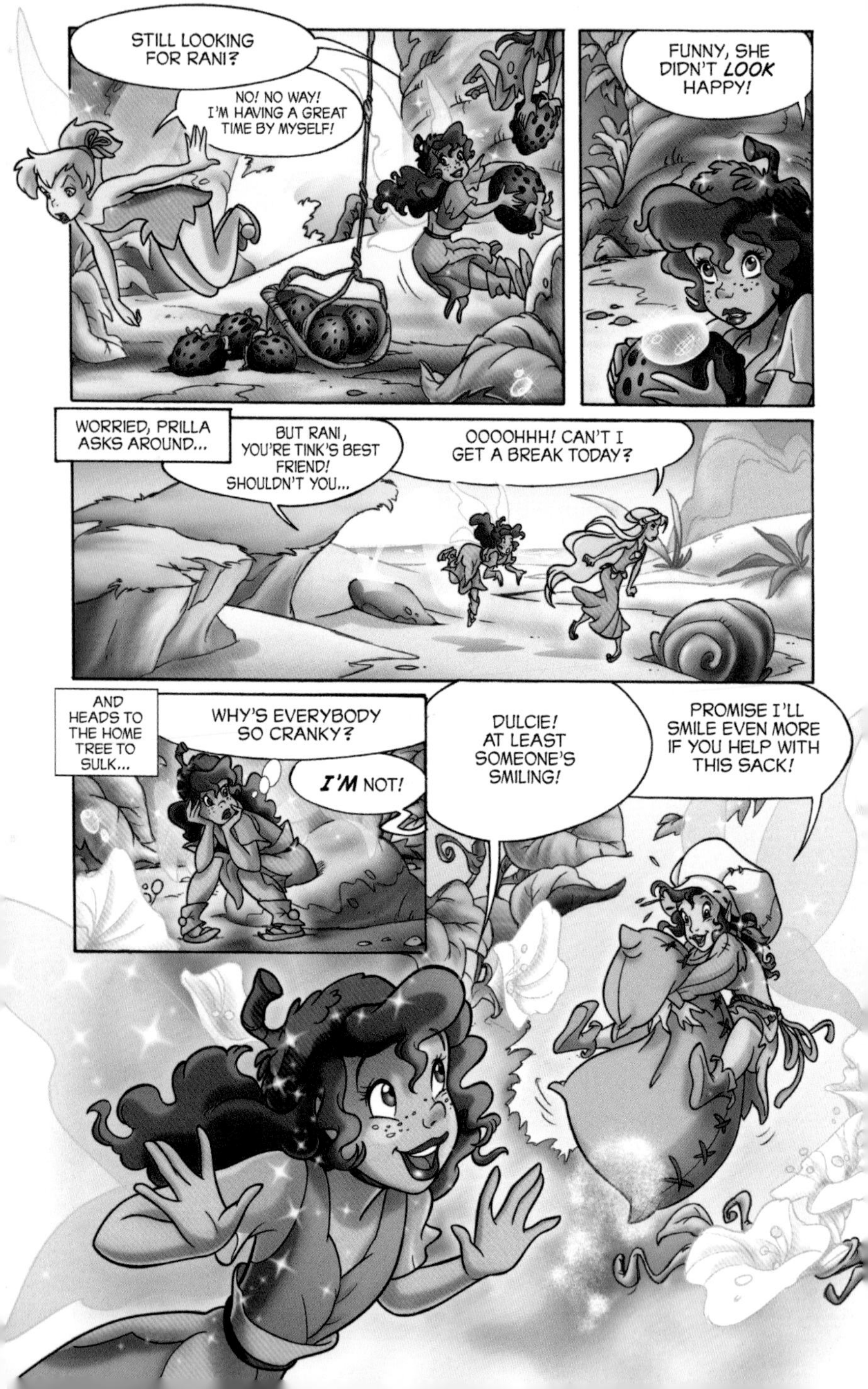
STILL LOOKING FOR RANI?
NO! NO WAY! I'M HAVING A GREAT TIME BY MYSELF!
FUNNY, SHE DIDN'T *LOOK* HAPPY!
WORRIED, PRILLA ASKS AROUND...
BUT RANI, YOU'RE TINK'S BEST FRIEND! SHOULDN'T YOU...
OOOOHHH! CAN'T I GET A BREAK TODAY?
AND HEADS TO THE HOME TREE TO SULK...
WHY'S EVERYBODY SO CRANKY?
I'M NOT!
DULCIE! AT LEAST SOMEONE'S SMILING!
PROMISE I'LL SMILE EVEN MORE IF YOU HELP WITH THIS SACK!

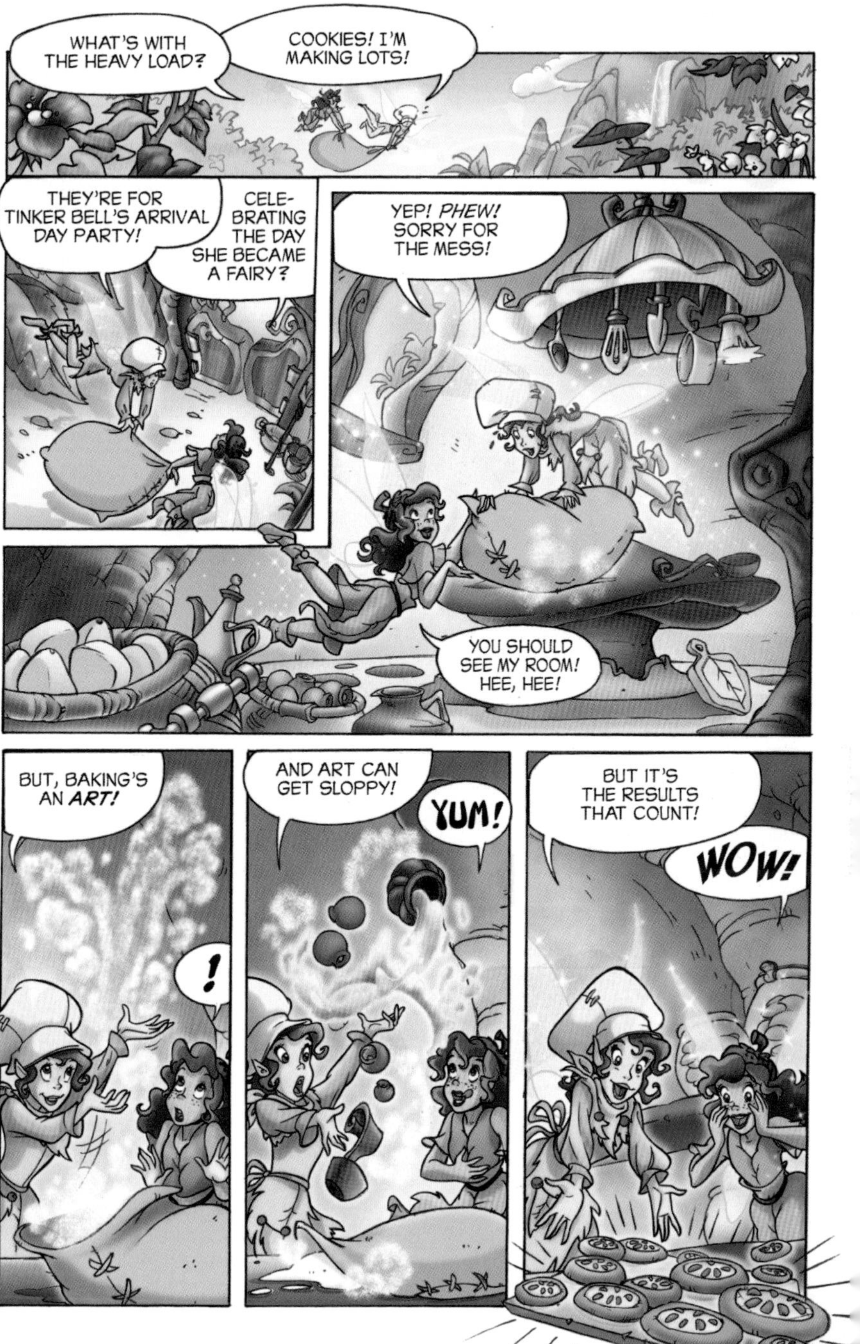

WHAT'S WITH THE HEAVY LOAD?
COOKIES! I'M MAKING LOTS!
THEY'RE FOR TINKER BELL'S ARRIVAL DAY PARTY!
CELE-BRATING THE DAY SHE BECAME A FAIRY?
YEP! *PHEW!* SORRY FOR THE MESS!
YOU SHOULD SEE MY ROOM! HEE, HEE!
BUT, BAKING'S AN ***ART!***
!
AND ART CAN GET SLOPPY!
YUM!
BUT IT'S THE RESULTS THAT COUNT!
WOW!

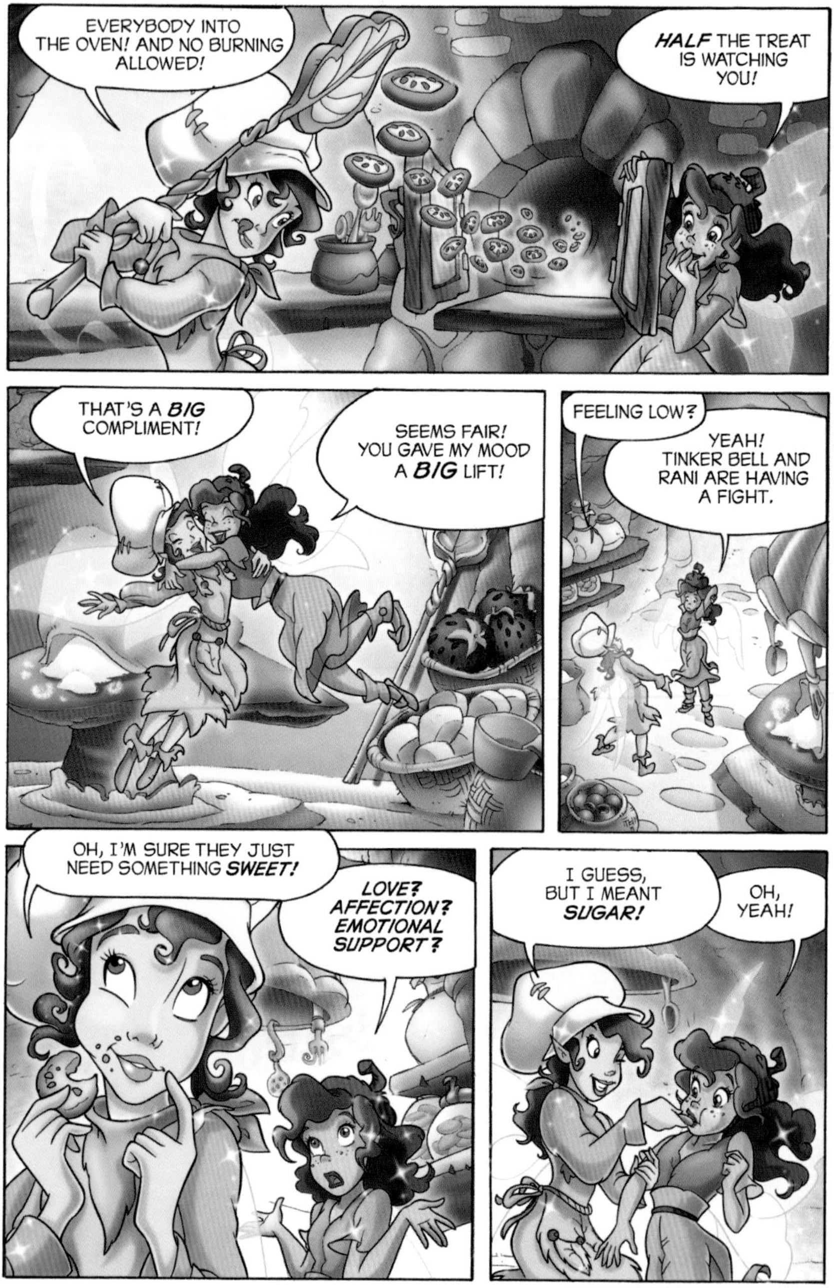
EVERYBODY INTO THE OVEN! AND NO BURNING ALLOWED!
HALF THE TREAT IS WATCHING YOU!
THAT'S A BIG COMPLIMENT!
SEEMS FAIR! YOU GAVE MY MOOD A BIG LIFT!
FEELING LOW?
YEAH! TINKER BELL AND RANI ARE HAVING A FIGHT.
OH, I'M SURE THEY JUST NEED SOMETHING SWEET!
LOVE? AFFECTION? EMOTIONAL SUPPORT?
I GUESS, BUT I MEANT SUGAR!
OH, YEAH!

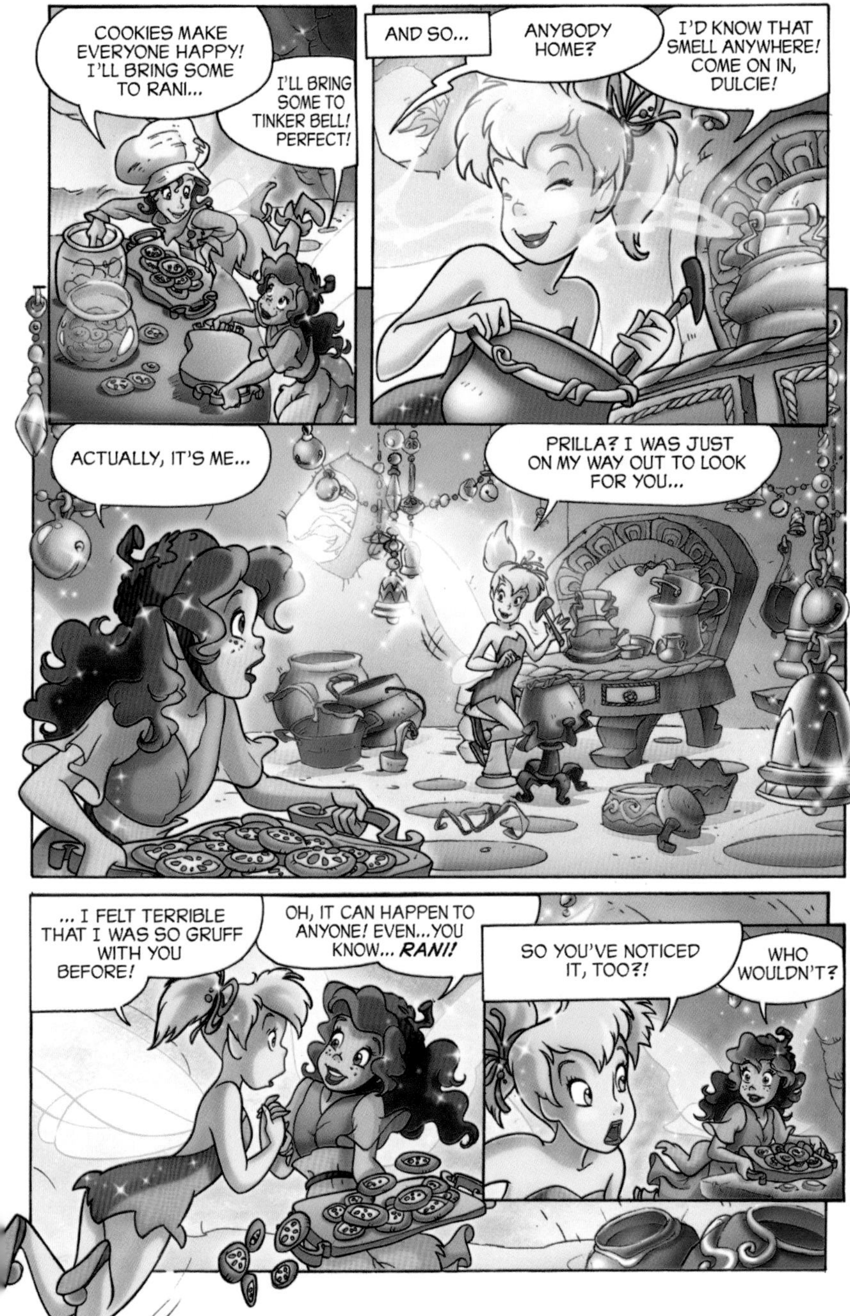
COOKIES MAKE EVERYONE HAPPY! I'LL BRING SOME TO RANI...
I'LL BRING SOME TO TINKER BELL! PERFECT!
AND SO...
ANYBODY HOME?
I'D KNOW THAT SMELL ANYWHERE! COME ON IN, DULCIE!
ACTUALLY, IT'S ME...
PRILLA? I WAS JUST ON MY WAY OUT TO LOOK FOR YOU...
... I FELT TERRIBLE THAT I WAS SO GRUFF WITH YOU BEFORE!
OH, IT CAN HAPPEN TO ANYONE! EVEN...YOU KNOW... RANI!
SO YOU'VE NOTICED IT, TOO?!
WHO WOULDN'T?

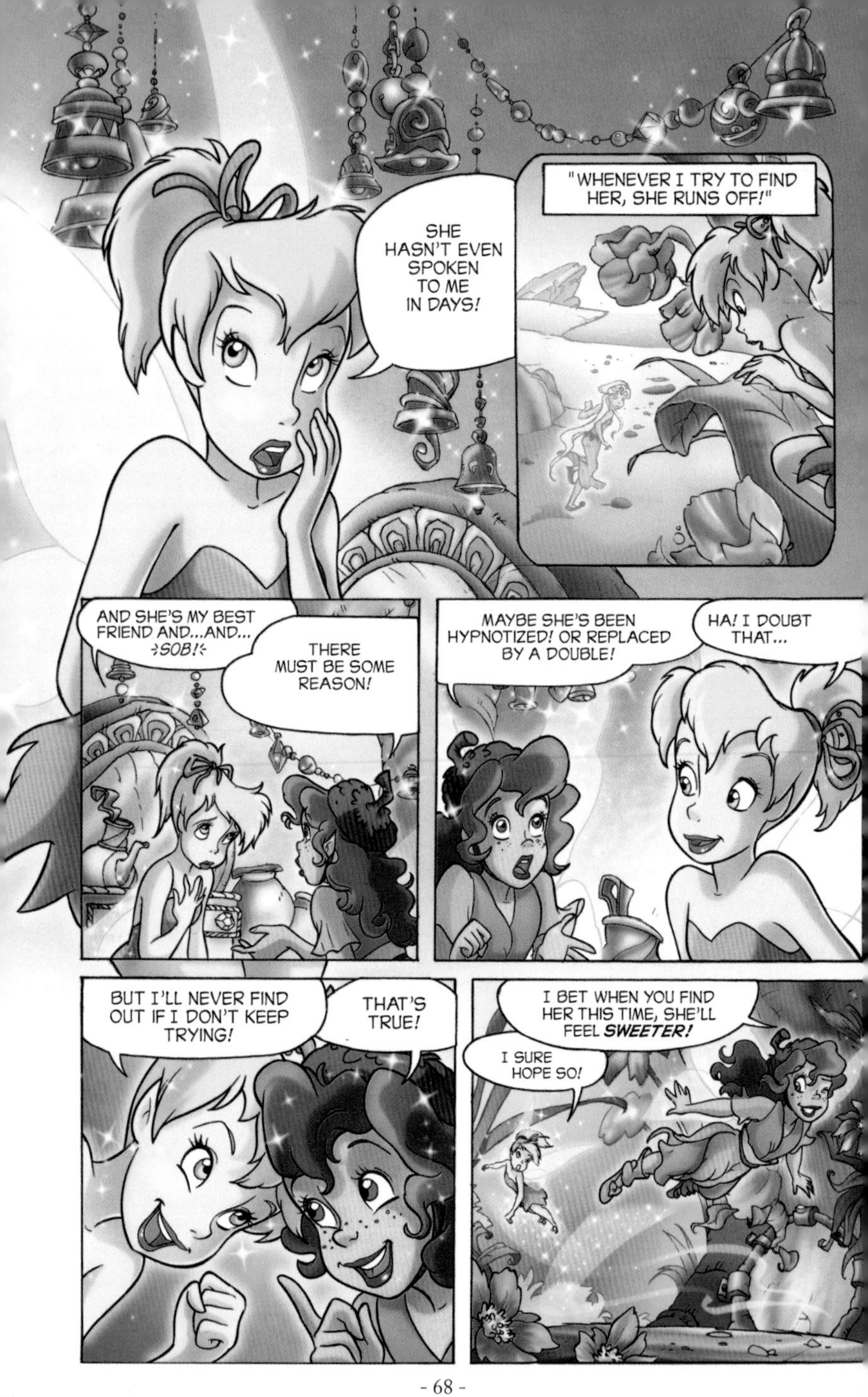
SHE HASN'T EVEN SPOKEN TO ME IN DAYS!
"WHENEVER I TRY TO FIND HER, SHE RUNS OFF!"
AND SHE'S MY BEST FRIEND AND...AND... SOB!
THERE MUST BE SOME REASON!
MAYBE SHE'S BEEN HYPNOTIZED! OR REPLACED BY A DOUBLE!
HA! I DOUBT THAT...
BUT I'LL NEVER FIND OUT IF I DON'T KEEP TRYING!
THAT'S TRUE!
I BET WHEN YOU FIND HER THIS TIME, SHE'LL FEEL SWEETER!
I SURE HOPE SO!

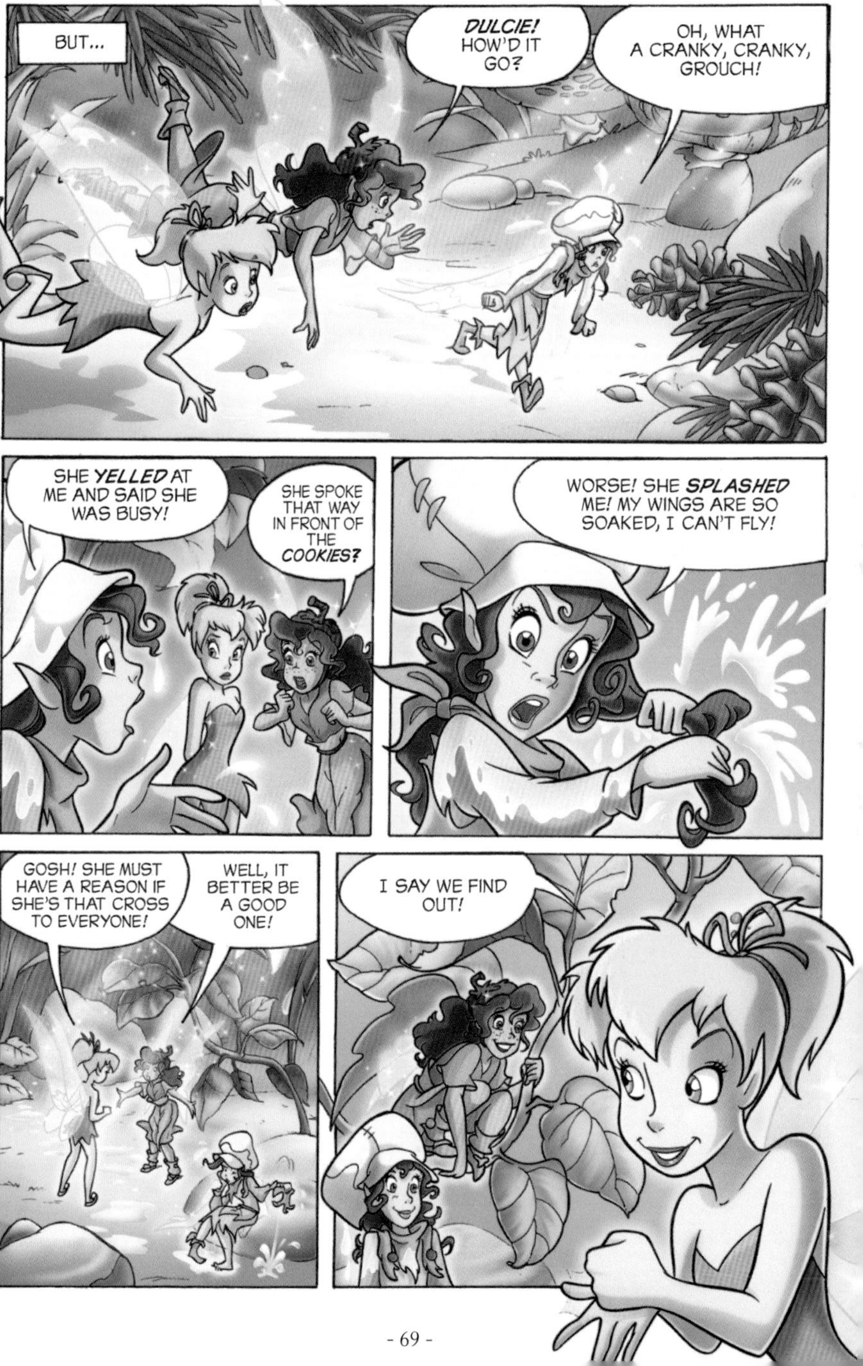
BUT...
DULCIE! HOW'D IT GO?
OH, WHAT A CRANKY, CRANKY, GROUCH!
SHE YELLED AT ME AND SAID SHE WAS BUSY!
SHE SPOKE THAT WAY IN FRONT OF THE COOKIES?
WORSE! SHE SPLASHED ME! MY WINGS ARE SO SOAKED, I CAN'T FLY!
GOSH! SHE MUST HAVE A REASON IF SHE'S THAT CROSS TO EVERYONE!
WELL, IT BETTER BE A GOOD ONE!
I SAY WE FIND OUT!

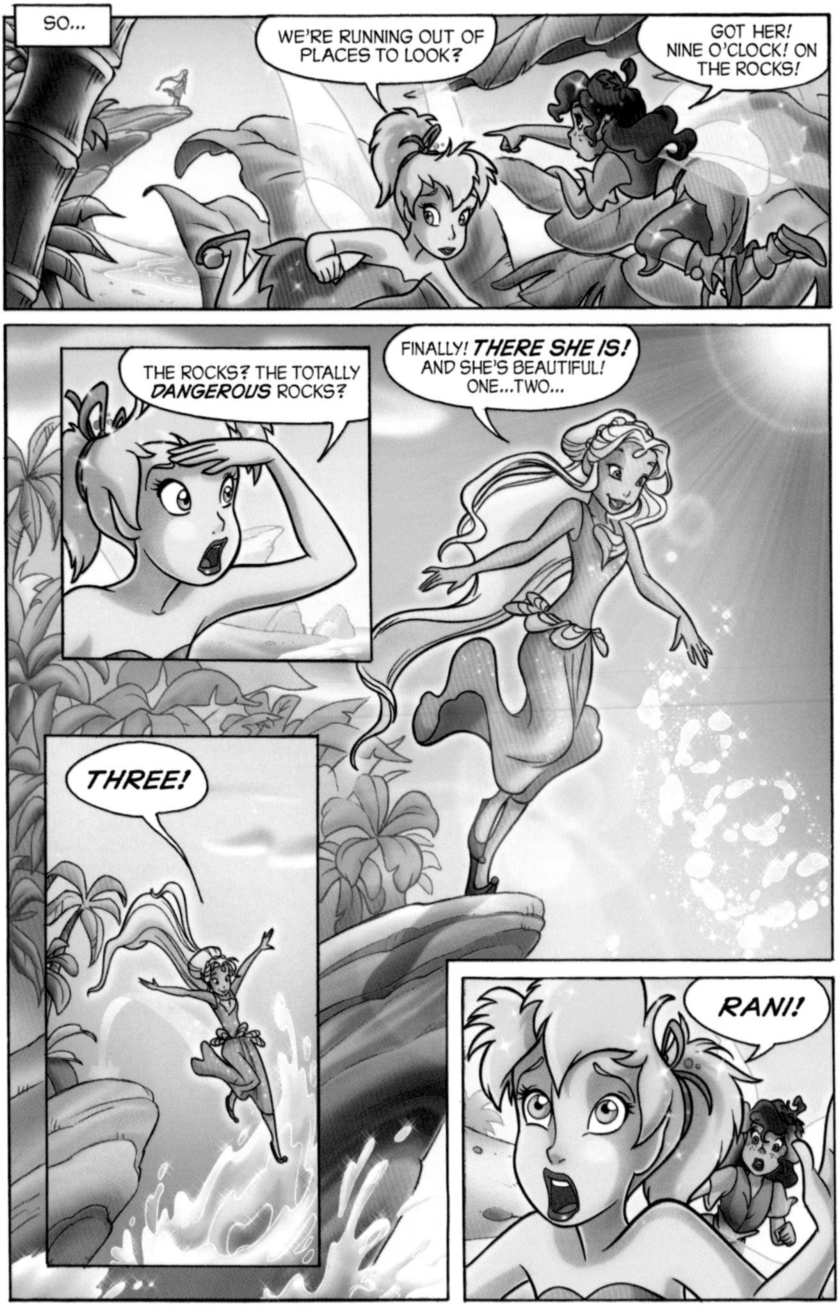
SO...
WE'RE RUNNING OUT OF PLACES TO LOOK?
GOT HER! NINE O'CLOCK! ON THE ROCKS!
THE ROCKS? THE TOTALLY *DANGEROUS* ROCKS?
FINALLY! ***THERE SHE IS!*** AND SHE'S BEAUTIFUL! ONE...TWO...
THREE!
RANI!

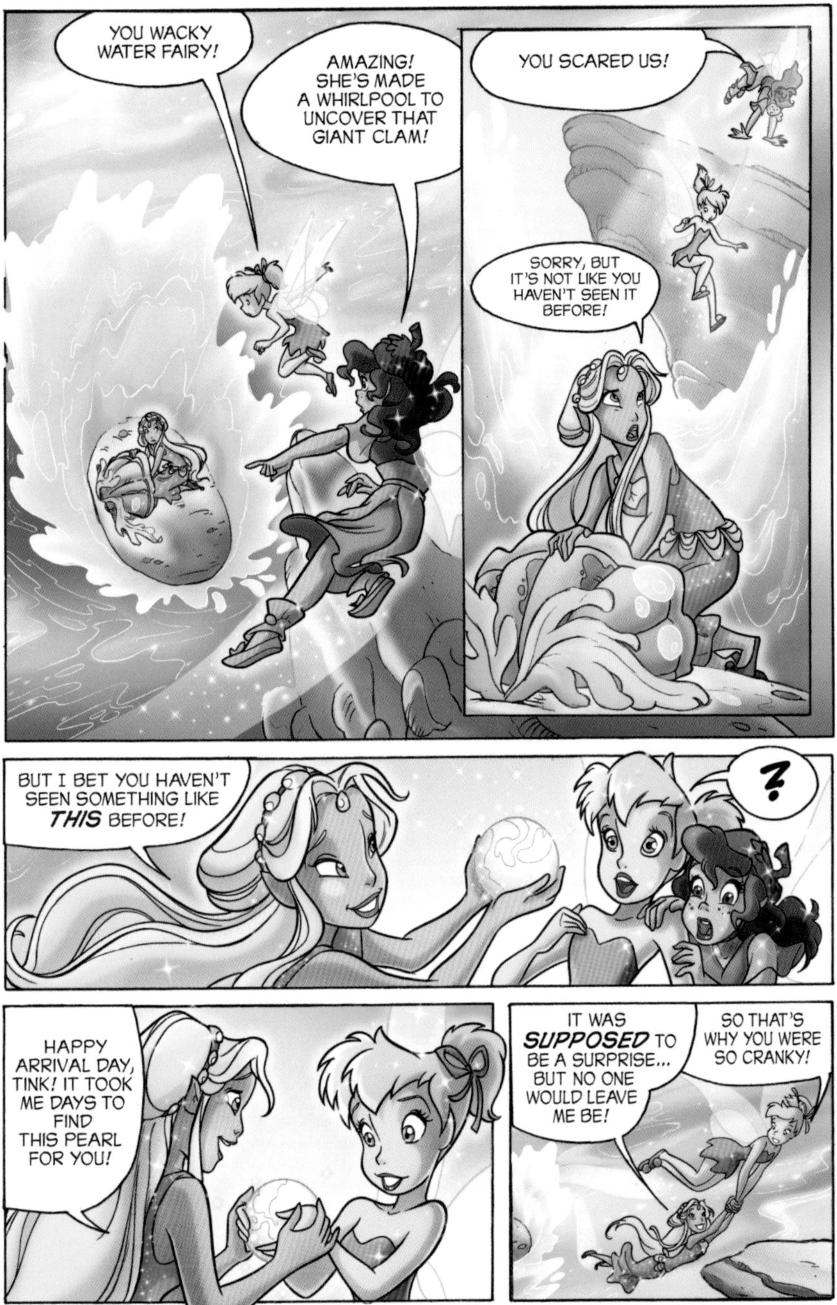
YOU WACKY WATER FAIRY!
AMAZING! SHE'S MADE A WHIRLPOOL TO UNCOVER THAT GIANT CLAM!
YOU SCARED US!
SORRY, BUT IT'S NOT LIKE YOU HAVEN'T SEEN IT BEFORE!
BUT I BET YOU HAVEN'T SEEN SOMETHING LIKE *THIS* BEFORE!
?
HAPPY ARRIVAL DAY, TINK! IT TOOK ME DAYS TO FIND THIS PEARL FOR YOU!
IT WAS *SUPPOSED* TO BE A SURPRISE... BUT NO ONE WOULD LEAVE ME BE!
SO THAT'S WHY YOU WERE SO CRANKY!

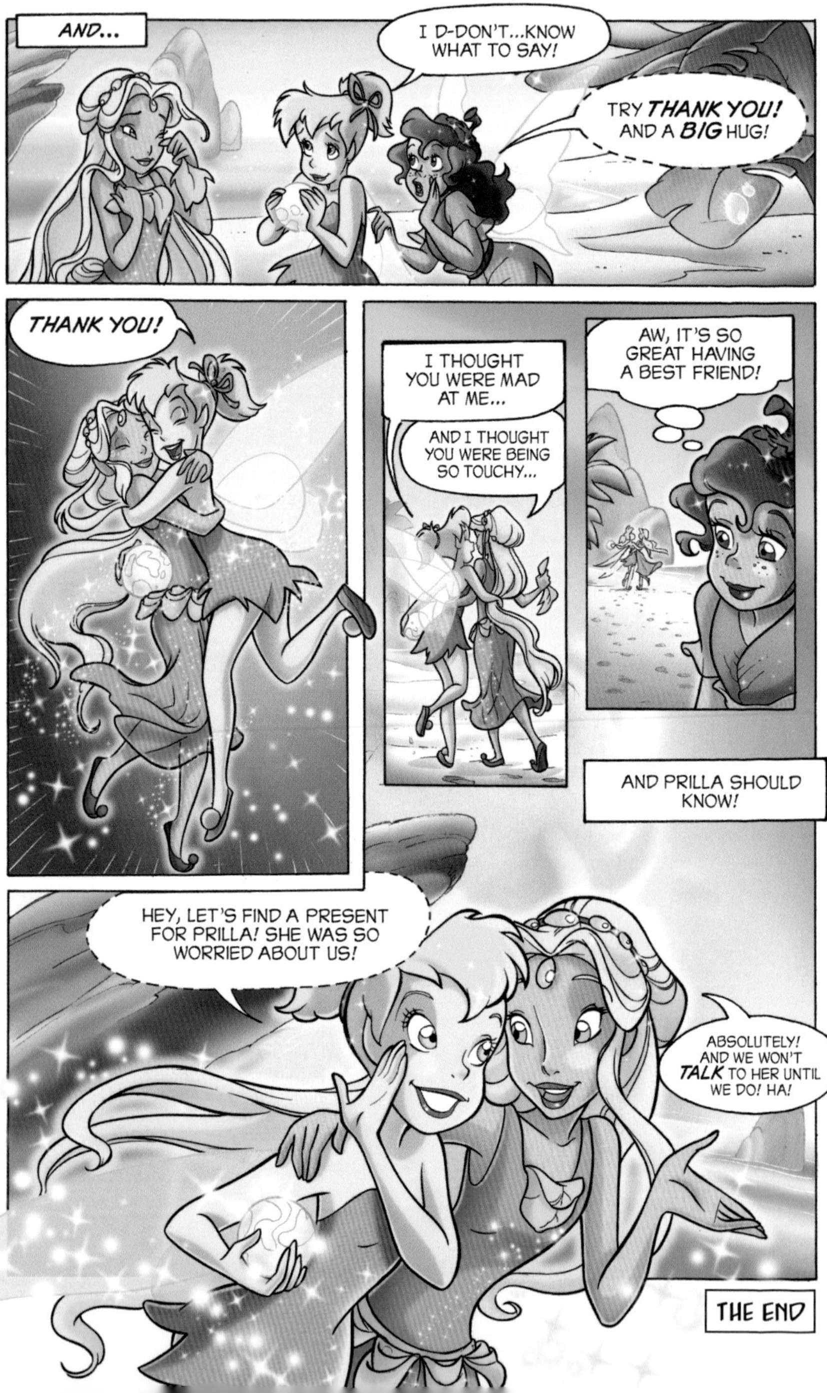
AND...
I D-DON'T...KNOW WHAT TO SAY!
TRY THANK YOU! AND A BIG HUG!
THANK YOU!
I THOUGHT YOU WERE MAD AT ME...
AND I THOUGHT YOU WERE BEING SO TOUCHY...
AW, IT'S SO GREAT HAVING A BEST FRIEND!
AND PRILLA SHOULD KNOW!
HEY, LET'S FIND A PRESENT FOR PRILLA! SHE WAS SO WORRIED ABOUT US!
ABSOLUTELY! AND WE WON'T TALK TO HER UNTIL WE DO! HA!
THE END

NANCY DREW

WATCH OUT FOR PAPERCUTZ™

It's official! Papercutz has finally published a real, honest-to-Goofy Disney graphic novel, and we couldn't possibly be happier!

In the past, Papercutz has indeed published the adventures of ZORRO, the legendary hero who starred in the wonderful TV series produced by Disney, and of course, we're still publishing THE HARDY BOYS, who were featured in a serialized adventure on the classic Mickey Mouse Club TV series a long, long time ago. But now, Papercutz is proud to be working directly with the wonderful folks at Disney to bring you DISNEY FAIRIES comics! We especially want to thank Tonya Agurto, Tishana Williams, Ivonne Feliciano, Jesse Post, and Shiho Tilley for their support and awesome efforts.

Before I forget, I should introduce myself—I'm Jim Salicrup, the Editor-in-Chief at Papercutz. Terry Nantier and I started Papercutz five years ago to help create more comics suitable for readers of all ages. We're proud to publish such graphic novel series as NANCY DREW, BIONICLE, CLASSICS ILLUSTRATED, GERONIMO STILTON, THE HARDY BOYS and more! At the back of our books, we try to provide a peek at some of our other titles, bring you the latest Papercutz news, and feature interviews with our artists and writers. This time around we thought we'd offer a look at one of the stories in CLASSICS ILLUSTRATED DELUXE #2 "Tales From the Brothers Grimm." So, on the following pages, enjoy Philip Petit's adaptation of "Hansel and Gretel."

To find out more about Disney Fairies, you can go online to www.disneyfairies.com. For more about the DISNEY FAIRIES graphic novels, go to www.papercutz.com.

And don't miss DISNEY FAIRIES Graphic Novel #2 "Tinker Bell and the Wings of Rani"— an all-new, book length adventure, coming soon. Until next time, keep believing in magic!

Thanks,

JIM

Special Preview of "Hansel and Gretel"
from CLASSICS ILLUSTRATED DELUXE #2
"Tales From the Brothers Grimm"

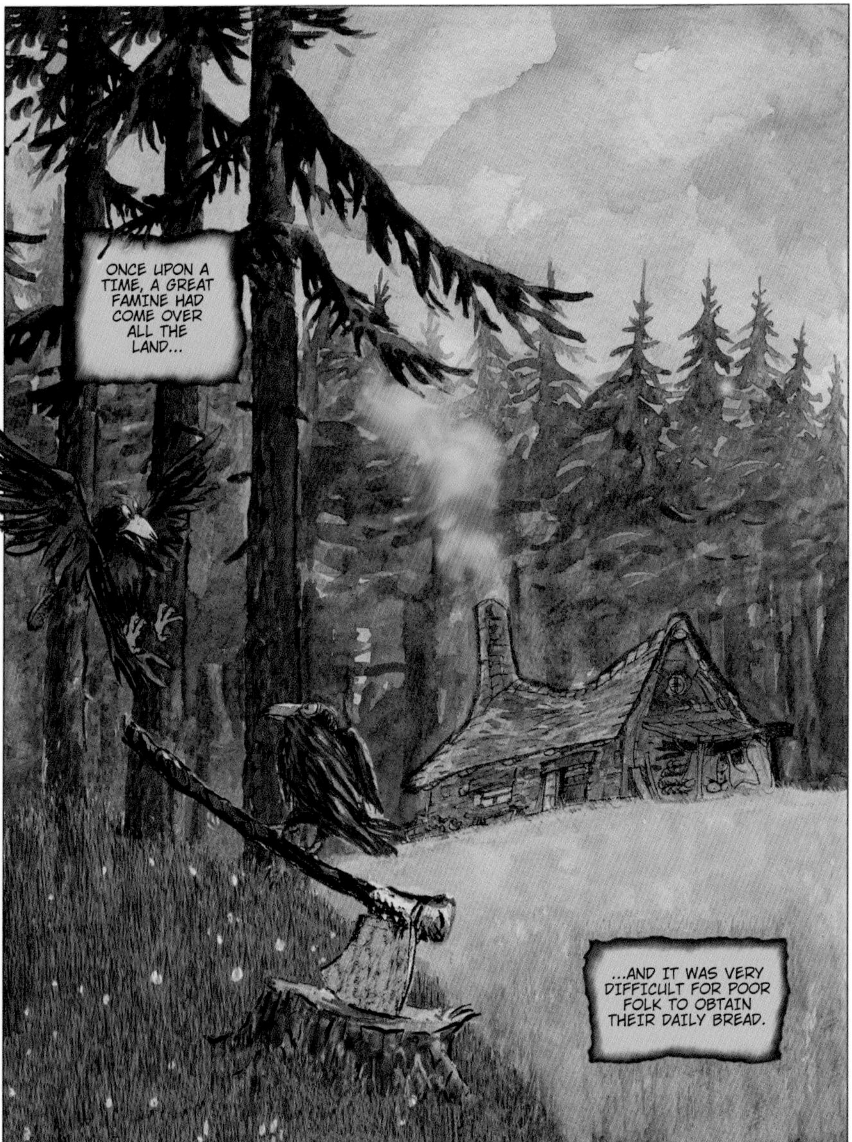
ONCE UPON A TIME, A GREAT FAMINE HAD COME OVER ALL THE LAND...
...AND IT WAS VERY DIFFICULT FOR POOR FOLK TO OBTAIN THEIR DAILY BREAD.

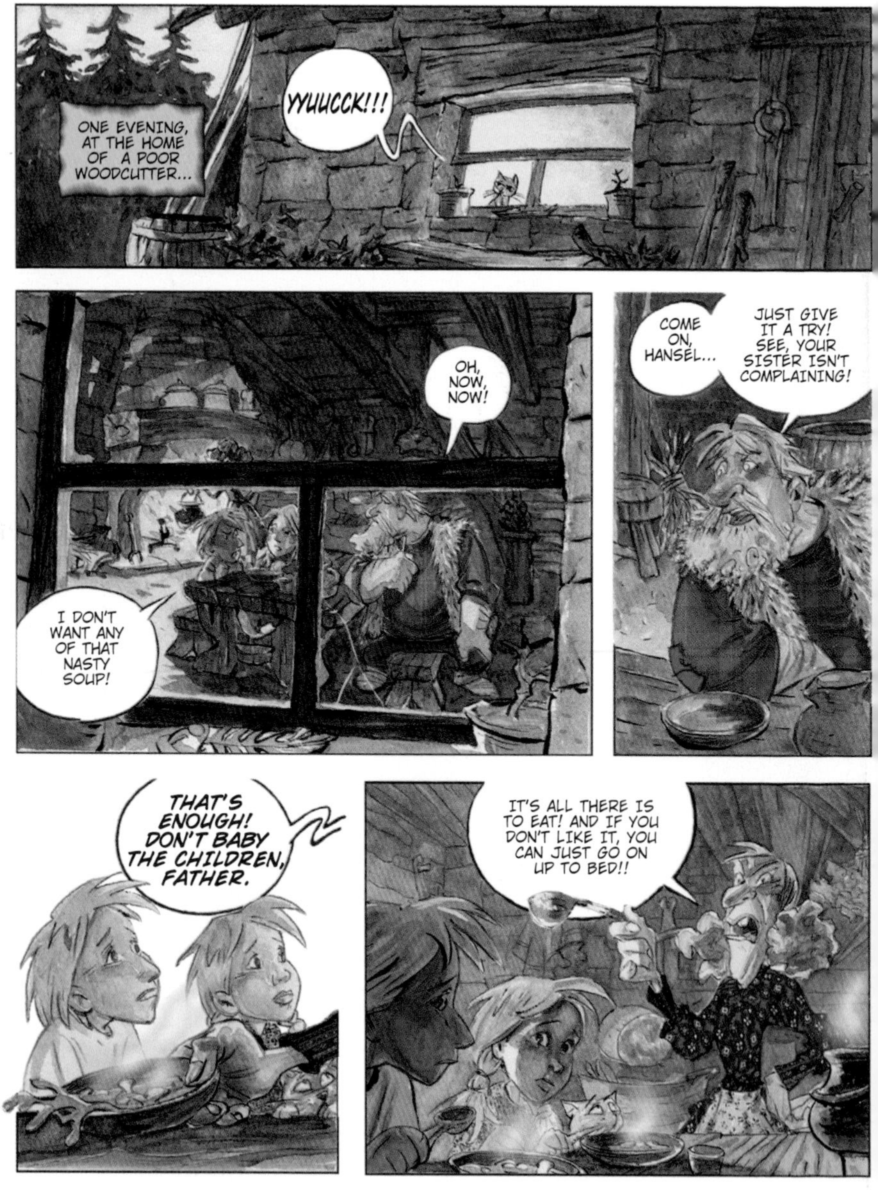
ONE EVENING, AT THE HOME OF A POOR WOODCUTTER...
YYUUCCK!!!
OH, NOW, NOW!
I DON'T WANT ANY OF THAT NASTY SOUP!
COME ON, HANSEL...
JUST GIVE IT A TRY! SEE, YOUR SISTER ISN'T COMPLAINING!
THAT'S ENOUGH! DON'T BABY THE CHILDREN, FATHER.
IT'S ALL THERE IS TO EAT! AND IF YOU DON'T LIKE IT, YOU CAN JUST GO ON UP TO BED!!

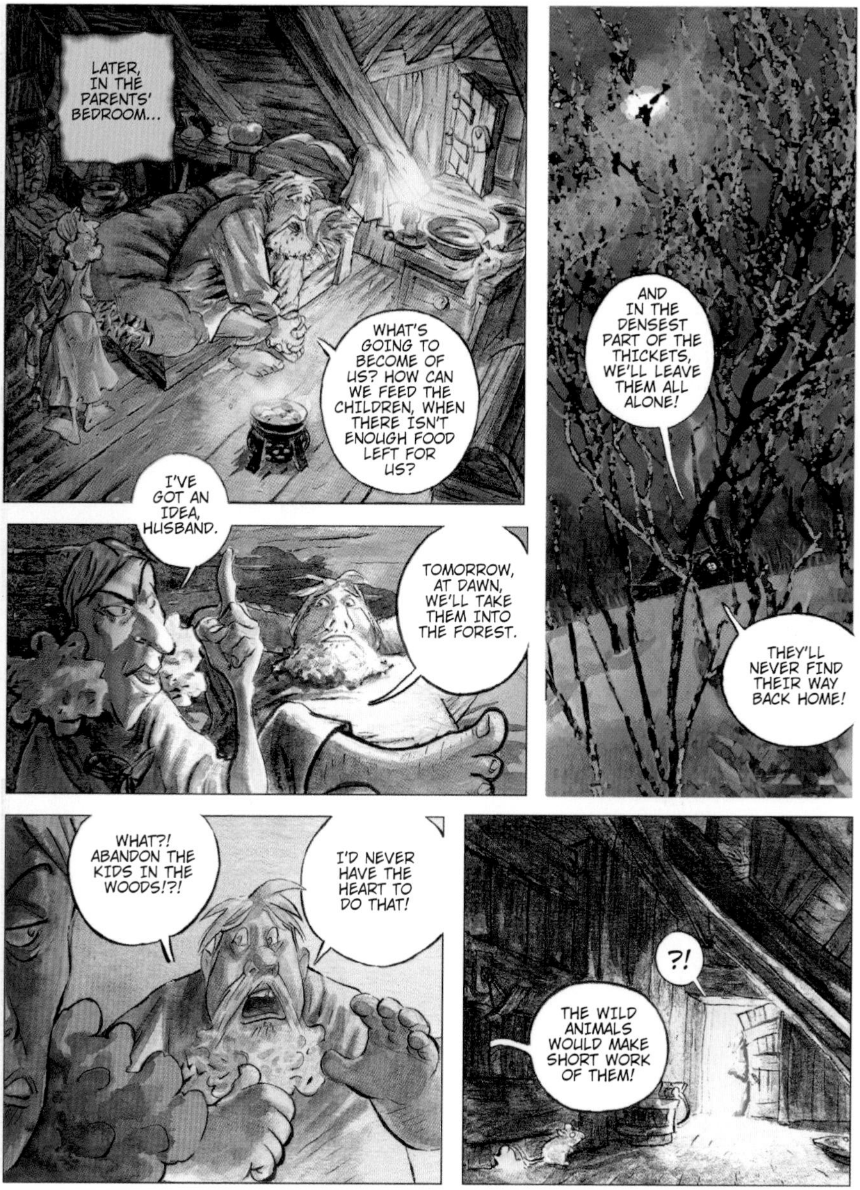
LATER, IN THE PARENTS' BEDROOM...
WHAT'S GOING TO BECOME OF US? HOW CAN WE FEED THE CHILDREN, WHEN THERE ISN'T ENOUGH FOOD LEFT FOR US?
I'VE GOT AN IDEA, HUSBAND.
TOMORROW, AT DAWN, WE'LL TAKE THEM INTO THE FOREST.
AND IN THE DENSEST PART OF THE THICKETS, WE'LL LEAVE THEM ALL ALONE!
THEY'LL NEVER FIND THEIR WAY BACK HOME!
WHAT?! ABANDON THE KIDS IN THE WOODS!?!
I'D NEVER HAVE THE HEART TO DO THAT!
?!
THE WILD ANIMALS WOULD MAKE SHORT WORK OF THEM!

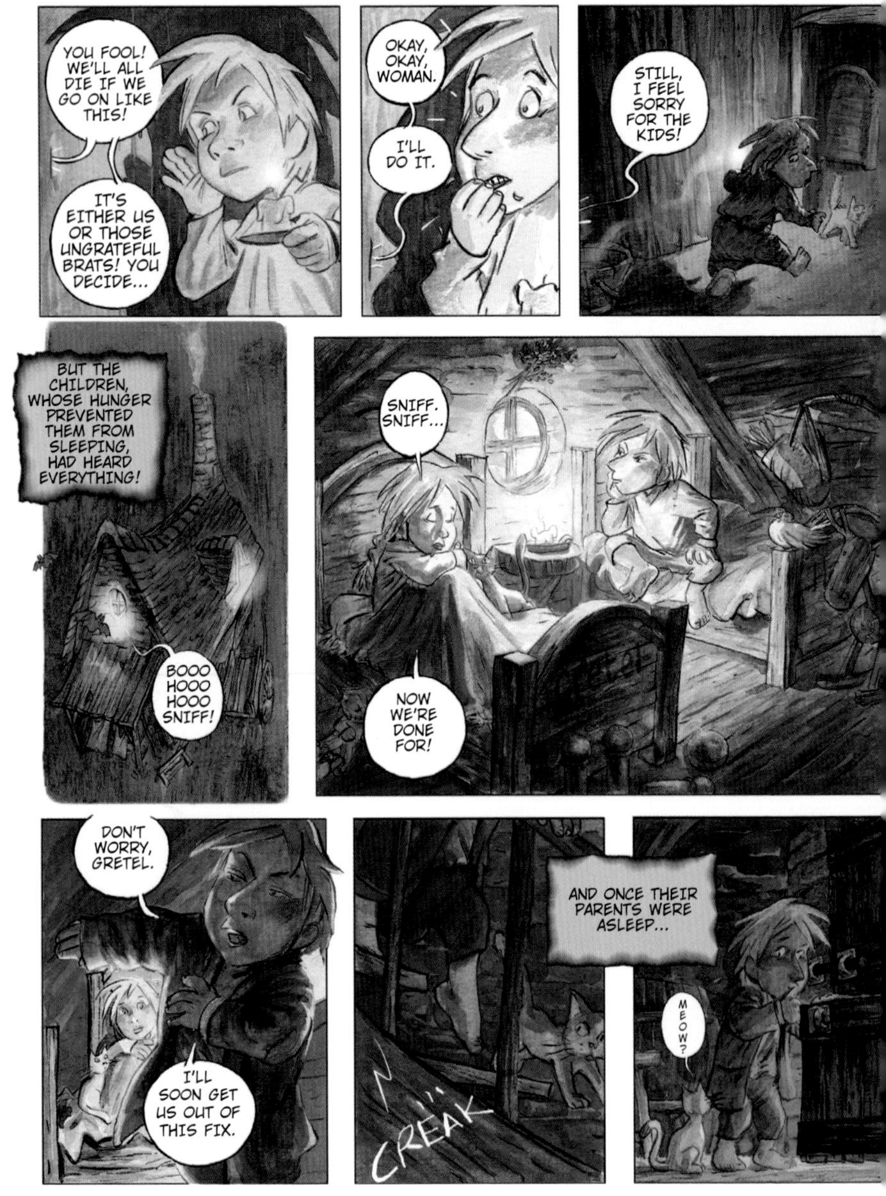
YOU FOOL! WE'LL ALL DIE IF WE GO ON LIKE THIS!
IT'S EITHER US OR THOSE UNGRATEFUL BRATS! YOU DECIDE...
OKAY, OKAY, WOMAN.
I'LL DO IT.
STILL, I FEEL SORRY FOR THE KIDS!
BUT THE CHILDREN, WHOSE HUNGER PREVENTED THEM FROM SLEEPING, HAD HEARD EVERYTHING!
BOOO HOOO HOOO SNIFF!
SNIFF. SNIFF...
NOW WE'RE DONE FOR!
DON'T WORRY, GRETEL.
I'LL SOON GET US OUT OF THIS FIX.
CREAK
AND ONCE THEIR PARENTS WERE ASLEEP...
MEOW?

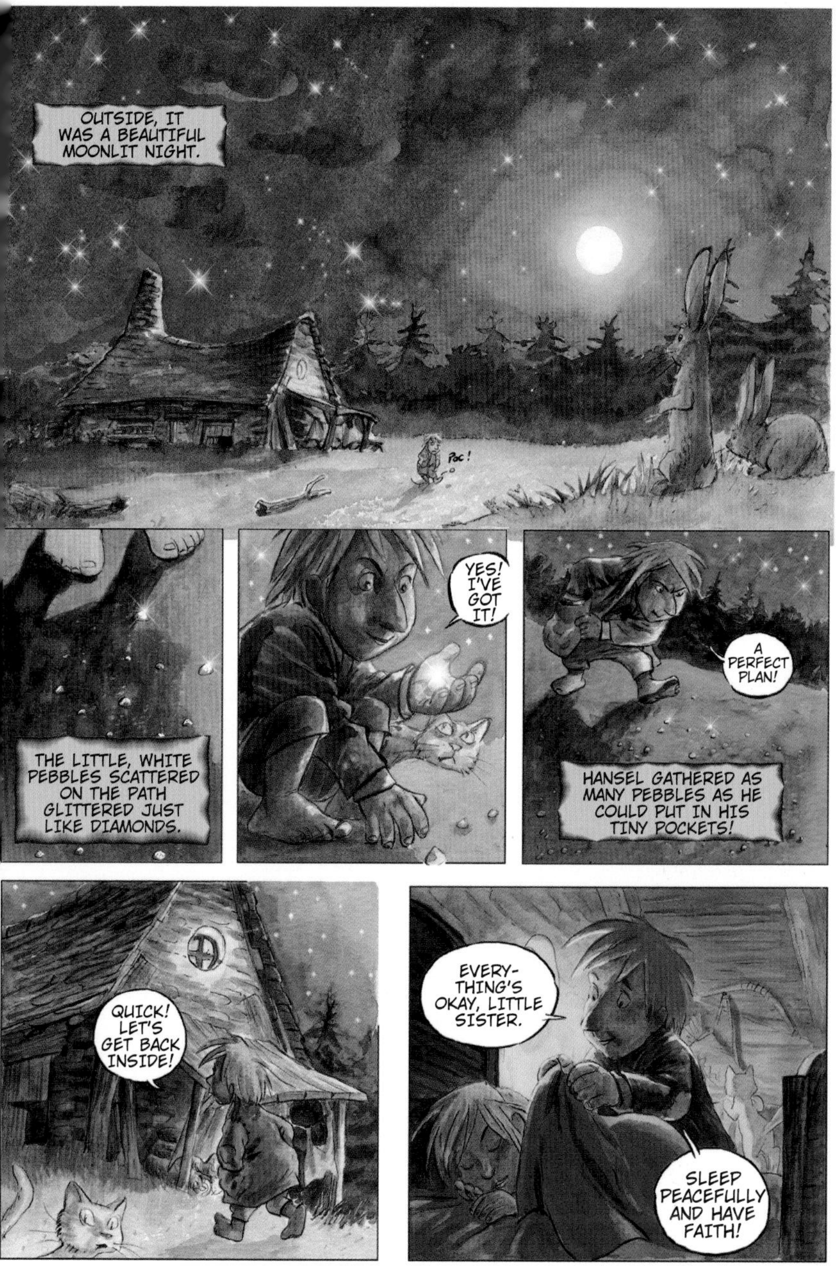
OUTSIDE, IT WAS A BEAUTIFUL MOONLIT NIGHT.
POC!
THE LITTLE, WHITE PEBBLES SCATTERED ON THE PATH GLITTERED JUST LIKE DIAMONDS.
YES! I'VE GOT IT!
A PERFECT PLAN!
HANSEL GATHERED AS MANY PEBBLES AS HE COULD PUT IN HIS TINY POCKETS!
QUICK! LET'S GET BACK INSIDE!
EVERY-THING'S OKAY, LITTLE SISTER.
SLEEP PEACEFULLY AND HAVE FAITH!

Continued in CLASSICS ILLUSTRATED DELUXE #2
"Tales from the Brothers Grimm" on sale now.

Discover the stories of Tinker Bell and her fairy friends!

COLLECT THEM ALL!
Available wherever
books are sold.
Also available on audio.

www.randomhouse.com/disneyfairies
www.disneyfairies.com